Phantom Holiday

The small Devonshire hotel where reporter Jim Larkin arrived to spend an out-of-season holiday was quiet – too quiet. In perfect order, with beds made up, tables laid, a turkey stuffed ready for the oven, but empty of staff and guests. No one in the village knew what had become of the proprietor and his wife and the girl who worked for them. When their disappearance persisted and the nationals got on to it, it was soon headlined as 'the *Mary Celeste* on dry land'.

Was it a publicity stunt, designed to revive a dwindling tourist trade? The local police seemed to think so and implied that Larkin was in on the act. The owners of the rival hotel also seemed suspect. Were they in collusion or had rivalry flared into something worse? It was left to Larkin, with his reporter's instinct, to probe the mystery more deeply – almost to the point of losing his life. Martin Russell's talent for the thrillingly unexpected has seldom been better displayed.

CRIME WAVE
DOUBLE HIT
CONCRETE EVIDENCE
ADVISORY SERVICE
DEADLINE
HUNT TO A KILL
DANGER MONEY
NO RETURN TICKET
NO THROUGH ROAD

Phantom Holiday

Martin Russell

76 46904

The Crime Club
Collins, 14 St James's Place, London

William Collins Sons & Co Ltd
London . Glasgow . Sydney . Auckland
Toronto . Johannesburg

First published 1974
© Martin Russell, 1974
ISBN 0 00 231639 0
Set in Monotype Baskerville
Made and Printed in Great Britain by
William Collins Sons & Co Ltd Glasgow

CHAPTER I

THE REVOLVING DOOR spun Larkin into a reception area
of modest size. The carpeting was battered, but a
welcoming shade of claret. Warm waves swam from a
radiator across the airspace in front of the tiny counter
at the foot of the stairs, announcing their opposition to
mid-April. Larkin looked for a bell.

Presently he coughed.

To his left as he faced the counter, a glass-panelled
door was labelled 'Lounge and Dining-room'. Through
it he could see deep chairs scattered about low tables on
a carpet of subtle purples and greens. He eyed them
appreciatively.

The place was going to suit him.

An old-fashioned latch arrangement secured the door.
Lifting it, he put his head into the room to be greeted by
the scent of woodsmoke. Remnants of a log fire smould-
ered in a metal basket inside a vast inglenook of rough
brick that occupied much of the right-hand wall and
served as a setting for a display of copper and pewter
implements, of dubious function, hung from the black-
oak surround. Beyond the inglenook in a corner, the
entrance to a passage bore the 'Dining-room' label, plus
one that cautioned 'Mind Your Head'.

Closing the door, Larkin returned to the counter to
cough again.

Then he noticed the bell. One of the hand-swung
variety on a shelf to the right of the counter. Reaching
for it, he applied a tentative waggle.

The outcome made him jump. Hurriedly he jammed

it down, organizing some facial muscles for the Larkin Smile (Half-Special) that looked like being needed; wondering resentfully where the bell had started its existence—in a nearby chapel belfry? It should have stayed there. He leaned on the counter, rubbing his eyes.

It had seemed a long drive. Reflecting ruefully on the supposedly recreational nature of his trip, he asked himself what would have been wrong with the train. Then he remembered. No trains. Because no railway. The road itself staggered only as far as the town before dying, which was largely why he had agreed that the place might be for him. All the same, it had seemed a long drive.

Again he left the foyer. This time he crossed the lounge and walked stoop-shouldered through the dim passage to the dining-room. A pleasant room at the end of the inn, windowed on two sides. He noted the five neatly-laid tables with their upturned glasses and their folded serviettes, glanced approbatingly from a window at the hillside view, inspected the typed menu— cream of asparagus soup, lamb cutlets or roast turkey, followed by pear Hélène or cheese and biscuits—and retraced his steps, faintly cheered, to the still deserted foyer and from there via the revolving door to the street, where he scanned the porch fabric for a bell-push.

After a few moments he found one, camouflaged by a stem of japonica throwing itself across stonework and timbers. He gave it a jab that produced no detectable result.

He stepped back to examine the upper windows. Seeing nothing of interest, he lowered his gaze to the main street.

Some distance along on the opposite side stood

another hotel. The Royal. Its aspirations to majesty, he calculated, were those of a pretender. The façade was painted a deep and dirty cream; a concrete canopy above the main entrance was supported by a couple of chipped pillars in fluted cement. Larkin was glad to be booked in at the Stag. He took another look inside, then re-emerged to stand irresolute, looking for life.

Little was evident. Some distance beyond the Royal, a woman was vanishing into a shop; a dog trotted diagonally across the road and shot into an alley. The remaining activity was limited to the passage of a lorry from one end of the main street to the other, where it dropped several gears to take a bend and laboured out of sight and earshot. Larkin contemplated the scene. Hacking sounds came from a nearby butcher's: walking along to it, he opened the door to the toll of a gong and descended two steps to the flagstoned floor.

'I'm sorry to trouble you, but do you happen to know what time there'll be somebody around at the Stag?'

The butcher stopped hammering at a piece of steak to consider both Larkin and the question.

'Summ'un around?'

'I can't seem to find anyone at the moment.' Larkin smiled his helpless smile.

The butcher, a man as thickset and bloodshot as one of his own joints, threw the steak accurately into the centre of a square of greaseproof paper and stood staring at it.

'Tried ringing?' He stressed the middle g.

Larkin laid claim to having rung. 'The one outside, and a handbell in the foyer. I don't believe anyone's there.'

'Should be,' said the butcher, having estimated this. 'You wantin' to stay there, like?'

'I've a room booked.'

'Aar. You wander back there, then, give 'em another shout. They's around somewhere.'

'Not on the ground floor.' Larkin watched the meat papered into a cube and secured with a gummed price-tag. 'I shouted up the stairs, but nobody came.'

The butcher slid the cube skilfully to join a pile of similar cubes and scratched into his hair.

'Likely they'll be down the basement. Trouble wi' the boiler maybe.'

'Just the two of them, is it—Mr and Mrs Sanderson?'

The handbell, opined the butcher with a certain leery caution, should have aroused Maisie.

'Maisie?'

'Sort of helper, she is. Serves at table an' that.'

Larkin said he would go back and scout around for Maisie.

'Give 'em another blast of the 'andbell,' advised the butcher, grinning wickedly. 'Case they're snorin' away the afternoon, like.'

The street was as desolate as ever. Walking back to his parked MG sports two-seater, Larkin collected his suitcase from the rear cavity and spun himself back into the Stag's foyer, clasping the luggage to his chest. Fetching up with some violence against the counter, he reached for the handbell and gave it a bold double shake.

Echoes shouted back.

Replacing it, he straddled the suitcase with his legs, arranged both forearms across the counter's grained surface and wondered idly whether the nearest bathroom would prove to be within dodging distance of his room or at the remote end of a groaning passage past five doors and a linen closet. The point wasn't crucial. The important thing was to gain primary admittance. He tried another cough. He drummed the woodwork. Leaving the suitcase, he reconnoitred once more the lounge area: this time, to the right of the passage, he found a door which opened into a large kitchen one step down.

An entire turkey, dressed and stuffed ready for the oven, sat in a metal tray on a working surface. He studied it with interest. No other eatables were in sight. A rack of sparkling plates stood near by. The room was cooler than the rest of the inn. Descending the step, he crossed to the outer door, the glass of which was shrouded by transluscent plastic, and opened it to reveal an extensive cobbled yard flanked by what had once been stables. To his immediate left was a brick-built one-story annexe to the inn; facing him, inside an open section of the stable structure, stood an elderly Morris Minor Traveller with dented wings. Larkin took a pace or two out on to the cobbles.

'Hullo there?'

He withdrew to the kitchen, closing the outer door meticulously behind him. Mouth muscles at the ready, he returned to the passage, walked back into the lounge and through to the foyer. His suitcase, sagging at the corners, sat where he had left it. With a shrug he picked it up, carried it outside, threw it into the MG, locked the car and went for a walk.

Half an hour later there were people in the foyer.

At his arrival they swung about. A couple in their middle years and a teenage girl. The man, whose eyes bulged like an entranced rabbit's, took a step towards him, two-thirds timid and a third aggressive.

'We've been trying to make someone hear.'

'They're an elusive crowd,' Larkin told them pleasantly. 'I gave up and went for a walk.'

'Aren't you the manager?'

'If I were, I'd be a bit concerned about the efficiency factor. What I'd like to be is a guest.'

'Us too,' observed the woman. Her eyes bulged like her husband's. Larkin was fascinated by this. Had like called to like, or was proximity to blame? 'We've rung and we've shouted and there's not a sign of anybody. I suppose they're at tea or something.'

'All at once?' The man consulted his wrist. 'I don't reckon wasting any more time here. There's another place, isn't there, along the road?'

'The Royal.'

'Come on, girls. We'll try that.'

'Good luck,' said Larkin.

At the revolving door the man turned. 'Not going to hang about, are you?'

'I'm supposed to be booked in here.'

'Oh. Well, best of luck to you, then. Looks like you'll need it.'

The eyes of their daughter bulged as well. For a moment Larkin thought about this, wondering whether his and Bunty's son or daughter would inherit his own creased countenance or Bunty's tip-tilted nose. Bringing children into being, he thought gloomily, was a hell of a lottery. His watch said nearly five. Gaining acceptance into the Stag Inn was, it appeared, likewise a lottery. One in which he was at present the loser. Irritation surged. He smote the counter with a fist. 'Hullo!' he roared.

Nobody came.

CHAPTER II

THE ROYAL's receptionist was a thin-faced girl with straight dark hair and an unexpectedly charming smile that she used sparingly upon the bulge-eyed family while they booked in.

Larkin hovered. Despite his walk he felt mentally congested; to think was an exertion. Perhaps Feldham was right, he did need this holiday. A tiny hump-shouldered porter doubled himself further beneath the family's luggage: they pursued him to the lift. Larkin stepped forward.

'I wonder, can you tell me anything about the Stag Inn?'

The smile came and quickly went. 'It's one-star, sir, with seven rooms. If you wanted to—'

'I'm sorry, I didn't mean that. It's just that I've been trying to find someone to attend to me there and the whole place seems deserted. Is it usually like that in the afternoons?'

The girl sent a glance towards the family, now vanishing behind lift doors.

'They mentioned something about finding nobody there. Have you tried—'

Yes, said Larkin, he had rung the bells. 'And coughed and knocked, all the usual things. I'm afraid I've run out of ideas.'

'We can offer you a room here.' She ran a pencil down a page. 'We've a nice—'

'But I'm booked at the Stag, you see.'

'Oh.'

'For a week.'

'A *week*! That's different. I wonder why you can't get an answer . . . Would you like me to try phoning them for you?'

'I'd be most grateful.' He hoped his expression was the beam he intended and not the leer he suspected.

After a while she put the receiver down with a frown.

'It's not like them. Either Mrs Sanderson or her husband is always on hand, somewhere within call— then there's Maisie, she's there till dinner's finished. What's the time now? Five-fifteen. They're bound to be back soon. Have you come far?'

'London.'

'If you'd like to wait here, I could get you a pot of tea.'

'Seems a bit cool,' said Larkin, 'as I'm staying at the rival establishment.'

The smile flickered. 'We don't carry it to extremes. Both family firms, you see: all very friendly. It's like that in this town. If you don't mind sitting over there, I'll have a tray brought through.'

'Most kind of you. Have you a public phone?'

She pointed to a cubicle under the stairs.

Bunty's voice sounded tinny. She said, 'Oh love. You've chosen the very instant I've got cheese melting over toast under the grill and green lacquer dripping from an ornament. Wait while I call Aunt Dodie . . .' Offstage noises boomed in Larkin's ear. 'I'm back. Sorry about that. How's the West Country?'

'A long way to the left of Hertfordshire.'

'What sort of town is it?'

'Tomblike. End of the road, literally. Everything Alan said of it.'

'Nice scenery?'

'Good walking country, from what I've seen. Tell you about that in due course.'

'While I'm sponging your blisters. Don't try to cover more than twenty miles a day, will you? You can kill yourself, relaxing too hard. What are the Sandersons like?'

'So far I've not run them to earth. At this instant I'm in the other hotel, the Royal, about to quaff a cup of their—'

'What the heck are you doing there?'

'Killing time while the Stag gets back into its stride. So far I've been here an hour and I haven't managed to contact anyone yet.'

'I didn't catch that.'

He explained. Bunty marvelled briefly. 'Gone shopping, I expect. When you do meet up with them— Is that the third tenpence you've put in?'

'Yes, and I've no more. So now I know that you and Auntie D. are battling along amid the cheese and the lacquer and that you're feeling okay . . . You are feeling okay?'

'Thanks,' she said indignantly, 'for asking. I think I am. Aunt Dodie keeps pushing me down into armchairs and telling me to watch the box or get knitting. I don't want to knit. You'd think Junior was due tomorrow, you'd think—'

'You do what Auntie says. She's strong as a horse, you've always said so, thrives on work, so grab what you—There go the pips again. 'Bye now, all my love. I'll phone tomorrow.'

A tray of tea and biscuits had been placed on a circular table in the reception area. Pouring himself a cup, he sat back with it and sighed.

His eyes scanned other chairs for discarded news-

papers. Then he remembered what Feldham had said·
He made his body sag. Drank slowly. To the second cup
he added extra sugar, because of what they said about
the effect on metabolism of lengthy motorized journeys.
He ate a biscuit. The humped porter spilled himself out
of the lift, threw an arch remark to the receptionist and
dived behind a screen. Larkin waited in vain for further
diversion. Rising, he went to the desk.

The girl took his money with a smile of greater
duration than hitherto.

'Like me to try the Stag again for you?'

'I'm sure it's not necessary. I'll walk back and simply
wait for someone to show up.'

'Remember,' she said, 'we've got vacancies if you're
stuck.'

A second look at the town persuaded Larkin that this
was barely surprising. He wondered at Feldham's
having found it to his taste; until he remembered the
angling. Equipped with a rod, his partner would have
lodged cheerfully for a month in a riverside shed.
Larkin, whose fishing tastes were of a more abstract
nature, gazed along the main street—now peopled by
a tiny boy and a tinier girl outside a sweetshop—zipped
his sheepskin jacket against the cutting breeze and
returned to his parked car. He was trying to insert the
wrong key in the door lock when a woman of about
sixty appeared in the Stag's porch, regarding him
anxiously.

'You're not anything to do with the inn?'

'I'd like to be,' he informed her. 'There's a room
awaiting me, I hope. Are you staying here?'

'I'm looking for my sister.' The worry in her face
intensified. 'I've been ringing since three o'clock, but
no reply. Where she is I can't imagine.'

'Mrs Sanderson, you mean?'

'No, no. My sister works for them. Just mornings. She helps with the rooms. She should have been home by two. Four at the latest, if she had shopping to do.'

Larkin looked at her in silence. Pocketing the car keys, he joined her in the porch.

'What's the time now?' she asked.

'Twenty to six. I take it you've called and so on?'

'I've not only called, I've been to all the rooms looking for someone—anybody. The place is like the grave.'

Larkin said he knew what she meant. 'It was recommended to me as somewhere quiet, but I wasn't warned of anything quite like this. I suppose as they've very few guests at the moment—'

She shook her head.

'They've never that many. Not these days. They don't leave it empty, there's always someone on duty as far as I know. Anyhow, what about my sister? She'd have let me know . . .'

Her voice sounded tearful. He took her arm.

'Let's try again, both of us.'

'I've been all over—'

'Basement?'

'No, but they wouldn't all be—'

'Trouble with the boiler, the butcher suggested. How do we get down there?'

Meekly she took him through to the kitchen and pointed to what had seemed to be a cupboard door. 'There.' Her eyes roamed. 'Turkey all stuffed and waiting,' she said. 'It's on the menu for tonight, should have been roasting hours ago. Vegetables still in the freezer . . .'

Switching on a light, Larkin clattered down stone steps into an underground chamber, in the centre of which an oil-fired boiler hummed and vibrated. He eyed it for a moment. It gave every sign of trouble-free operation. Apart from some lengths of copper piping and a small stack of empty crates, the rest of the basement was void. After a few seconds of trance-like thought he returned upstairs to the kitchen. The woman was re-entering from the rear courtyard.

'Car's parked at the back,' she said tensely.

'That belongs to Mr Sanderson?'

'They both use it, I think Hilda said.'

'Well, at least they can't have had a motor accident. How does your sister normally come and go?'

'If I don't need the car, she drives herself here. Otherwise she comes by bus.' The woman looked around distractedly. 'The eight-thirty in the morning and the one-thirty home. Or the three-thirty if she shops. She's never—'

'Is there one after that?'

'The five-thirty. But she's never—'

'How long does it take?'

'From my house? About twenty minutes.'

'You're on the phone at home?'

'Yes.'

Larkin glanced at the kitchen clock. It was ten to six. 'Wait a few more minutes, then ring to see if she's arrived. She may have missed the three-thirty.'

'She'd have let me know.'

He said patiently, 'Something may have prevented her. Meanwhile I'll take another look round. You've been into all the bedrooms?'

'I've put my head round all the doors . . .'

He left her at the counter with instructions to phone

16

just before six. Trudging upstairs, he began at the first door on the left.

There were three bedrooms each side of a carpeted corridor whose floor alternately creaked and sagged under his feet. A window at the far end admitted some light. A seventh bedroom in an attic was reached by a small steep staircase next to the window. Every bed was tidily made and counterpaned; on each washstand lay a wrapped biscuit of soap alongside a polished tumbler and a sheaf of paper towels. Two bathrooms stood side by side at the staircase end. Their tiled floors were waxed to a dangerous shine; bathware and ceramics glittered hygienically. Midway along the corridor between two of the bedrooms was the expected linen closet, its contents folded immaculately in heaps. Closing the door on them, Larkin stood in a frown of concentration.

From downstairs came the ping of the telephone bell. He descended to find the woman with the receiver clamped to an ear, staring at him. At last, hopelessly, she replaced the instrument.

'Do you happen to know,' he asked, 'where the Sandersons sleep?'

In the annexe, she thought. They walked through to the courtyard cobbles and approached the incongruously varnished door. Under the impetus of Larkin's knuckles it swung inwards, came to rest. They exchanged glances.

She said fearfully, 'Are you going in?'

He raised his voice. 'Mrs Sanderson—are you there?' He stepped inside.

The room was as untidy as the inn itself was impeccable. Twin easy chairs with attached footrests sprawled at angles to the lifeless electric fire; the crumb-

B

strewn carpet compounded a general air of hospitable casualness in which the solitary item of stark efficiency was the television set. It stood out like a gold-capped tooth. Although nothing was overtly dusty, a vague overall impression of blithe neglect communicated itself to Larkin. Lived-in, he decided, was the phrase. On a table lay a copy of *TV Times*, open at the previous evening's programme. Flanking it, an open box, partly depleted, of Cadbury's Dairymilk Chocolates. Across an arm of one of the easy chairs was draped the *Daily Express*, sports page uppermost. Its date was the previous day's.

A notepad on a dresser took his eye. Across it lay a felt-tipped pen; writing covered half the exposed sheet. Hesitantly he stooped to read. It was page two of a chatty note: the final sentence ran, 'So Ted rather thinks it may be some while before the various technicalities can be'—and there stopped. Larkin flipped the page: the letter was to 'My dear Madge,' and seemed to concern a projected bank loan. Guiltily he removed his hand.

Doors at the rear of the room opened into a tiny kitchen and a bathroom, both slightly unkempt: a third door stood next to the dresser. Pausing at it, he listened.

'Mrs Sanderson?' He cleared his throat. 'Mr Sanderson? Are you not well?'

After a further interval he lowered the handle and pushed back the door.

From outside: 'Any sign of them?'

The bedroom was as ordinary as the rest of the annexe. Plain twin divans with yellow quilts, an old mahogany wardrobe, an oblong mirror fixed to the wall. Opening the wardrobe door, he peered inside and shut it again. He went out.

On his way past the notepad he lifted the sheet a second time. The letter was dated the previous day. With a last look around he left the annexe, carefully reclosing the varnished door.

'Nobody there,' he told the woman.

Turning without a word, she hurried back into the inn. He followed, securing doors in his wake. In the foyer they found a pink-cheeked man in his fifties looking blankly up the staircase: he had driven, he told them, nine miles into town to buy farm tools and was hoping to dine at the Stag before driving home. Where was everyone? Larkin, voicing ignorance, advised a transference of loyalties to the Royal. 'In the meantime,' he added, discovering that it was six-twenty, 'I think we ought to tell somebody about this, don't you?'

The woman clutched at the counter. She spoke on the edge of a gasp. 'What's become of my sister?'

'Nothing, I'm sure,' said Larkin soothingly, 'that the others can't explain. Once they turn up.'

CHAPTER III

HE WAS DRYING his face with the coarsest of the Royal's towels when someone knocked. He opened the door to the slim receptionist.

'We've got Sergeant Willis downstairs,' she said apologetically. 'He wants to see you.'

'Tell him I'm damp.'

'He'll wait till you dry off.'

'Ask him to have dinner with me.'

'He doesn't eat on duty. Shall I say you'll be down?'

Larkin dolefully agreed to this. Fighting his way into a roll-necked sweater, he substituted a tweed jacket for his windcheater; his face tingled from its scrubbing, but journey fatigue sat on him like heavy grime. It was turned seven when he went dizzily downstairs.

'Sergeant Willis?'

'Yes, sir. You're the gentleman phoned us from the Stag?'

'Unfortunately. Shall we sit here?'

Their chairs were within view and hearing of the desk. The girl kept her gaze away. Sergeant Willis, a man as lean as Larkin and, he guessed, about his own age of forty-five, committed himself promptly once more to the leatherwork. 'Unfortunately?'

'Well, I came here for a rest. I'm supposed to be staying at the Stag.'

'Comfortable here.' Willis eyed the Royal's appointments.

'Oh, no complaints. But I was three hours messing around first.'

'Upsetting for you,' Willis said mechanically. 'Um, can you give me a statement?'

'I suppose so. Now?'

The sergeant nodded slightly and waited. Combating a desire to smash at him with a clenched fist, Larkin rendered an account of his arrival.

'Booked for a week, you say. When was the booking made?'

'About . . . twelve days ago.'

'By letter? And you had confirmation?'

Larkin showed him the typed acknowledgment on Stag-headed notepaper. Willis stared at the underlying scrawl.

'That Mrs Sanderson's signature?'

'I've no way of knowing. I took it to be.'

Retaining the exhibit, Willis settled back. 'Knew the Stag, did you, from some other time?'

'No, I didn't. My business partner recommended it. He stayed there three years ago.'

The seargeant nodded and seemed to remember something. He dragged out a notebook. 'I'd better have your full name.'

'James Larkin.'

'Occupation?'

'Journalist.'

A thin smile. 'Found yourself a story.'

'The germ of one,' Larkin agreed politely. 'Still no trace of any of them?'

With a glance at the receptionist, Willis leaned forward.

'Rummest business I ever met,' he confided. 'All in apple-pie order, not a pin out of place—only no staff. A knockout.'

'When were they last seen?'

The sergeant said cagily, 'We're still asking about that.'

The bulge-eyed family were into their main course as Larkin sat down. All three of them stared his way. Cursing soundlessly, he rose again, crossed to their table.

'As you see, I found my way here as well.'

'We gather they've not turned up yet.' The woman spoke with pleasurable condemnation through a mouthful of grilled steak.

'No. It's a mystery.'

'The service in some of these places is really shocking.'

'There's no spirit of obligation left,' pronounced her spouse. He was speedily reducing an omelet with the aid of a fork. 'They'll walk out, soon as look at you. What was that place we stayed last night?' ('The Queen's Head,' droned the daughter.) 'Know how long it took them to serve dinner? Hour and twenty minutes. I'm not exaggerating. These two waiters—'

'This particular instance,' said Larkin, 'seems to go somewhat beyond shoddy service.'

'I should say it does. To walk out and leave the entire place empty—'

'It's not clear whether they've walked out.'

'They might be in there somewhere, you mean?'

'Unlikely. Several of us have searched high and low. The police are there now, still looking.'

The family looked at each other.

'What an extraordinary thing,' said the woman.

Her husband laid down his fork. 'So they have walked out?'

Larkin shrugged. 'If so, their motive escapes me. The Sandersons own the inn, after all.'

He left them tossing this between them. An elderly waiter wearing an expression of fathomless melancholy took his order for a pork chop, collected surplus items of cutlery and hobbled away beyond one of the screens that the Royal seemed to grow, like synthetic hedges, in front of its interior doors. Larkin studied the dining-room. It faced the main street, now lamplit. There were twelve tables, each laid for dinner. He wondered when the rush would begin.

The soup made an appearance concurrently with a check-suited, portly man of late middle age, who made for the family's table and engaged them in hushed discourse. Larkin was assaulting the plate without zest (it was clear soup with noodles) when he found himself being similarly addressed.

'Mr Larkin? Philip Potter, the proprietor here. I hope you're being made comfortable?'

Assuring him on the point, Larkin mentioned the Stag.

'You were to have stayed there, I understand.' Potter said it without perceptible rancour. 'Their loss is our gain, but I find it inexplicable.' He sounded concerned. 'It's not like the Sandersons to let people down.'

'They may have mistaken the week,' Larkin suggested.

'But they wouldn't simply abandon the inn. It's unthinkable. Maisie and Hilda too.' Potter watched unseeingly the spoon enter Larkin's mouth.

'How old is Maisie?'

'Eighteen.'

'Does she drive a car?'

'She did pass her test, I do know.' Potter scraped his chin with a fingernail. 'But I don't know of any car.' A

23

thought seemed to occur to him: he examined it in silence for a while. 'You're thinking,' he added, 'she could have taken them all out somewhere?'

'Sergeant Willis said they'd be looking into all that. It seems unlikely to me. Someone would have seen them, for one thing. And if they'd—' Larkin stopped himself. 'Maisie doesn't live at the Stag?'

'No. With her aunt.' Potter indicated the other end of the main street. 'Is the soup to your liking?'

Larkin said something enthusiastic, thinking with anguish of the cream of asparagus that he might have been spooning away. As Potter showed signs of loitering, he said comfortingly, 'Later this evening they'll no doubt all reappear with a perfectly obvious and reasonable explanation. Perhaps they were taking a trip somewhere which Maisie and Hilda both forgot to mention. You've some attractive countryside here.'

Potter returned to him with a visible effort.

'We're rather proud of it. You're not planning to fish?'

'No, I'm no angler. I intend to walk.'

'I was going to say, the fishing's collapsed, you know. None to speak of for the past two years.'

'My partner did mention it. Pollution of some kind?'

'They built this plastics factory upstream.' Potter spoke with a curtness that was patently directed at the perpetrators of the outrage rather than at Larkin. 'Their waste material is discharged into the flow.'

'That seems terrible. I thought there were regulations—'

'Oh, they comply with them. Everyone says so. Local authorities, factory inspectors, the lot. The stuff's treated, filtered, diluted, de-toxined . . . they insist. All

24

we know is, the fish aren't to be had around here any more.'

'Something of a tragedy.'

'Hits us hard, of course. The trade, I mean. We relied on the anglers. As you know, this town's off the general motoring beat—drivers tend to carry on along the main road to Lifton or Launceston. There's nothing special to come to Miltham for, in itself. It was just handy for the fishing.'

Larkin commiserated. He wished the pork would arrive. Hunger was making him light-headed: all that the soup had done was to scratch at the raw surfaces of his stomach. He tore at a piece of bread. 'If motorists only knew,' he observed, 'they'd come here for the scenery.'

'Ah. But this is it. A place has to get known.'

'You'd think the anglers would have spread the word.'

A cynical smile struggled through the cloud mantling the other's face.

'Ever studied a fisherman? All he's interested in is finding the path to the nearest stream. Scenic beauty? He wouldn't know it from a sandworm. I've nothing against the rod and line merchants, mind. I'd like to see a few of them around again, believe you me.'

A younger version of Potter, wearing black curly hair and a polka-dotted bow tie, had appeared at the dining-room door. The proprietor excused himself. 'I must have a word with my son. Anything you need, Mr Larkin, let us know and we'll do our best for you.' He joined his son and they vanished into the foyer.

Larkin surveyed the tables with fresh vision. He was in, he reflected, for an even quieter time than he had foreseen, barring hourly visitations by policemen for statements. The elderly waiter hobbled past, bearing dishes. They contained peach Melbas for the bulge-eyed family. On his quivering way back to the screen he collected Larkin's soup plate and, before he could be prevented, the remains of Larkin's bread. Meeting the gaze of the woman, Larkin grinned encouragingly, watched the edge of her spoon bite into raspberry-topped ice and whipped cream.

He began to think unkindly of the Sandersons.

When at last the waiter staggered out with a serving dish, Larkin inquired how many more guests were expected. The old creature bent on him the scrutiny of a benevolent but depressed great-uncle.

'We're not expecting any, sir. April's a quiet time.'

'But I understand you're not exactly engulfed by tourists in any month?'

'Not now, sir, that's true. Of course we never did get the *tourists*. A little crackling, sir? The anglers were our great standby.'

'And now they've been driven off.'

The waiter's face betrayed nothing.

'You might say that, sir. It's progress, they tell me. The housewives must have their plastic wrappers.' An additional fold showed itself at one corner of the puckered mouth. 'Vegetables there, sir, if you'd care to help yourself. Apple sauce just here.' The waiter straightened, stood back to assess the table. 'In past years,' he said informatively, 'I've had a staff of four in here, and still we hardly knew which way to turn.'

'Times change.'

'They do, sir, they do indeed.' The waiter limped off. Larkin was taking up knife and fork when Potter returned to whisper that Chief Inspector Mossop was anxious for a word with him.

CHAPTER IV

'I SHAN'T keep you a single moment from your meal,' said the chief inspector, 'but I'd be most grateful if you could quickly give us a spot of help.'

Larkin said it was all right about the meal, Mr Potter had arranged to have it kept under warmers. Feeling weak, he squatted on the leather arm of a foyer chair. 'What can I tell you?'

'I've read your statement,' announced Mossop. 'Seems you were the first to actually notice anything amiss at the Stag. Between arriving and calling us, did you touch anything?'

'No. That is, I picked up the handbell by the counter and rang it. Otherwise, nothing.'

'The inn was in just the state it is now?'

'What state is it in now?'

Mossop smiled faintly. 'Dusted, swept, polished, provisioned, prepared. And not a soul inside.'

'Uncanny,' said Larkin, feeling that something was expected of him. 'When were any of them last seen?'

Mossop gave him a brooding glance. A square-faced man of short but powerful build, with iron-grey hair covering his head like the nap of a beaten carpet, he had the appearance of someone able humourlessly to take care of himself and also of anyone else who happened to be around. Larkin interpreted the glance. It meant that the chief inspector was asking the questions. He let it ride. Having taken his time, Mossop evidently decided that no harm had been meant.

'Hilda Cotteridge by her sister, when she left their

cottage at about eight-twenty. And half an hour later by several people as she walked through the town. Maisie by her aunt, soon after nine. Also by the newsagent whose shop she passes on her way along to the Stag: also by the butcher. The Sandersons—' Mossop gestured and was silent.

'Weren't they seen at all?'

'Not on present information, but apparently that's not so unusual. I'm told they're both sometimes busy inside the inn the whole morning.'

'What about tradesmen?'

'Milk was delivered early on—the usual way, down the side entrance to the kitchen door at the back—but the milkman says he saw nobody. Again, nothing out of the ordinary.' Mossop scowled. 'Thereafter it's a blank. Now you, Mr Larkin, had this week's booking starting from today. It's not possible you were notified they couldn't take you after all, and the notification never reached you?'

'Possible, I suppose. But in view of all the circumstances, unlikely, wouldn't you think?'

The chief inspector stared grimly at the reception desk.

'One has to eliminate,' he said presently. 'The theory might hold more water if they'd shut up shop, sent the two helpers packing—'

'They may have done that.'

'So where are they? Blind drunk the pair of them, celebrating their sudden freedom in some offbeat pub?'

'It's another theory,' Larkin said courteously. 'But it leaves a good deal unexplained.'

Mossop shifted restlessly. On apparent impulse he dropped into a chair to fix Larkin with a contemplative stare. 'You're a journalist, according to your statement.

I've seen stuff in the nationals by a James Larkin. Not yours, by any chance?'

'Could be. My partner and I run a small features agency which farms things out.'

'That mugging business in Herts a few months back. Place called Eden Village—'

'That was me.'

'Not bad,' said Mossop grudgingly.

'Thank you.'

'Came across quite nicely. Here on business, Mr Larkin?'

'For a rest. My partner thought I'd been overdoing it.'

Mossop nodded, and then meditated.

'In that case I'd best let you return to your dinner. But first let me ask you something.' He seemed to grope for words. 'In your job, you must have come into contact with a lot of crime. In this present instance, would you yourself say I'm making too much of it too soon? Tell me; I'm not proud. I can't quite decide what I'm faced with here. Could it be an elaborate practical joke?'

Larkin considered the thesis.

'My reply to that,' he said at last, 'would be that if it is, then they all deserve to come back to find policemen emptying cupboards and digging up stable floors. I take it this is what you're doing?'

'It's in the planning stage.' Mossop looked relieved. 'I don't want to make fools of myself and my chaps, but when all's said and done it's getting on for eight-thirty and four people are still missing . . . we have to take it seriously. I just wondered how it looked to an outsider.' He seemed to repent of his frailty. 'That'll be all, Mr Larkin, thanks. You'll be here overnight?'

'I intend staying for my original week, if possible.'

The chief inspector stood. 'By tomorrow you'll probably be able to move into your room at the Stag, where you're meant to be. I've a hunch they'll all show up before too long.'

Larkin said pleasantly, 'I trust you're right.'

After dinner he was glancing, from curiosity and indigestion, through the local weekly which he had found in a rack beside a radiator, when he intercepted the frank survey of the receptionist from behind the desk. He gave her a smile, a quarter-special. She responded with flattering immediacy.

'What d'you think of our *Thunderer*?'

'Nice job. Very bright for a weekly.'

'My brother-in-law edits it.'

'Is that so, indeed? From here in Miltham, or is it part of a group?'

'There's just a separate edition for Pettersley, he has to go out there now and then, but he's here most of the time. I'll tell him somebody admired his work.'

'I don't suppose he gets many tributes.'

'People take the local for granted, don't they? Unless it gets something wrong, then they raise the roof.' The girl paused. 'Sometimes,' she said casually, 'I give Smut stories.'

'What did you say?'

She chuckled. 'I don't mean what you thought I meant. That's what we call my brother-in-law, Smut. It comes from—'

'His ink-stained shirt-cuffs,' said Larkin.

'That's right! How ever did you guess?'

'I didn't have to. If I'm right, I worked with him once on a South Coast paper. His name's Gould?'

'Yes, it is. Fancy you knowing him.'

'It's five years ago.' He went across to the desk. 'There was a terrible outbreak of killings at the time, and it turned out that our crime reporter—'

'He's told me about that. And now I think of it—'

'Don't say,' said Larkin, pleased, 'he's mentioned me?'

'Yes he has, really. I didn't associate the name.'

He gave her an amused look. 'Either you've a good memory or you're the soul of tact. And what are these stories you pass on to him?'

'Oh—things I hear. You know. Items I pick up.' She looked embarrassed. 'Working in a hotel—'

He nodded understandingly. 'Central distribution points for rumour and gossip. What does your radar tell you about the current mystery?'

'The Sandersons, you mean? Oh, that's baffling. Nobody knows what to think. Personally I imagine it's some enormous mistake. A misunderstanding. All the same I've tipped off Smut, just in case.'

'Very wise.'

'He'd have known soon anyhow, he's got the police in his pocket. But he only arrived back from Pettersley half an hour ago, so I rang him then. He's probably at the Stag already.'

'Wrong,' said a familiar voice. 'He's inside the Royal, eavesdropping as usual. Hullo, Jim. Of all the places to meet up again.'

'I was right, then,' said Larkin, shaking hands warmly. Smut had materialized like a genie from behind a display of picture postcards to show himself as physically unchanged except for the better: he had shed a few facial corrugations and his former permanent expression of dread of incipient disaster. 'You're looking fine.'

31

'It's the rural life.' Smut examined him intently. 'That and the loving care of Irene's big sister, and I mean huge. As for you, Jim, candidly, I've seen you looking better. Too much booze, or not enough? I've been reading things about you.'

'Actionable, I hope.'

'Not half. I won't say what sort of action. Seriously, your progress has left me agape. Did you and Bunty—?'

'We did. And there's an addition to the family due in about two months from now.'

'Great. How many's that?'

'We're only just starting. Too much on the move till now.'

'Hear about it later. I'm off to the Stag. Coming?'

'Me? I'm on holiday.'

Smut stood off a pace to stare at him.

'This can't be Jim Larkin. The old model hadn't heard of holidays.'

'This one has. Though it can't deny that it's intrigued to know what—'

'That's better! See you, Irene. Thanks for the tip-off. Usual terms apply. Fill the glasses for when we get back.'

'I'll be away by then,' she said, smiling at Larkin and touching her dark hair.

'What staff do you have?' he asked Smut as they walked briskly through the breeze.

Smut raised both hands. 'These are my staff.'

'You do it all solo?'

'It's that sort of a sheet. Well, I can't put my hand on my heart and claim that I actually *print* it. We've a couple of ancient retainers to do that. For the rest, *la journal, c'est moi*. Quite restful. A far cry from the old *Review*.'

'You seem to enjoy it.'

'You're a loner yourself, Jim, so you'd understand.'

The Stag windows showed a light or two, but the porch was closed against them. Across the street, two youths and two girls sat astride a pair of motor-cycles, gazing at the building. Smut rang. After a while he rang again.

'They're immune to campanology around here,' Larkin explained.

The door opened to expose the head of a constable. At sight of Smut he moved himself aside.

'Might ha' guessed it was you. Chiefy's in the lounge. No, sir, sorry, you can't—'

'He's with me,' said Smut.

The constable fell back. Refastening the porch door behind them, he led the way through. The foyer was as blankly uninhabited as before. From upstairs came sounds of heavy footsteps. Inside the lounge, Mossop was talking to a small crumpled woman of late middle age with a mauve face and thin lips. Her sparse hair protruded in greyish wisps from beneath a faded green beret. At a sign from the constable, Smut and Larkin waited at a round oaken table under a window. Presently Mossop joined them.

'Maisie's aunt,' he muttered. 'A fat help.'

'I can imagine,' said Smut. 'I've had dealings with her. What's her theory about her niece?'

'Reckons she's gone off to spend the night with a fellow.'

'Feasible,' remarked Smut.

'Maybe, but wouldn't she have taken her coat?'

'It's still here?'

'Hung up behind the kitchen door. Next to Hilda's raincoat and scarf.'

'Tricky,' murmured Smut.

Larkin coughed. 'No clues?' he asked diffidently.

Mossop scowled at him. 'If I just knew,' he complained, 'what we were looking for. A girl missing . . . that's routine. A girl and a woman . . . dodgy. A girl, a woman, and both their employers, all leaving behind their outdoor garments in a hotel that's been spruced up and geared for action . . . this has got me beat. Where do I start?'

'At the beginning,' Smut said peacefully. 'I'm not abreast of the story yet.'

To Larkin's amazement, the chief inspector embarked docilely on an outline of the facts. Having heard them before, he gravitated towards Maisie's aunt, who observed his approach without excitement. He sat opposite her. Mossop glanced round but continued his exposition to Smut. Larkin took out his pipe and tobacco tin.

'Maisie,' he said, packing the bowl, 'likes a bit of fun, I dare say?'

The aunt's mouth clamped itself into a line that all but merged with her chin.

Producing matches, he created smoke. Settling back, he surveyed her with an authoritative air. 'You must feel disappointed when she lets you down like this.'

The mouth revealed itself suddenly by opening.

'Not the first time.'

'It's happened before?' he asked, watching the smoke.

The mouth snapped fast.

'This is slightly different though, isn't it? She and three others. And her coat left hanging in the kitchen.'

The eyes of Maisie's aunt flickered about the room. He sat still. Her mouth was reopening when Mossop intruded between them, Smut at his elbow.

34

'Mrs Charles here,' said the chief inspector tolerantly, 'takes the view that Maisie will show up again tomorrow.' He bent towards her. 'But what about Hilda Cotteridge, Mrs Charles?'

'Her an' all.'

'But where would she have gone? Her sister's not heard from her.'

'Mebbe she don't want her sister to know.'

'They've lived together for years. Why would she do that to her?'

'Better ask her, didn't you?' The mouth submerged and stayed under.

With a sigh the chief inspector straightened his spine.

'We shall, you needn't worry. But all this—' he turned to Smut—'only scratches at the main problem, which is the Sandersons. You know them a bit. Would you have said they're the type to go off at a moment's notice without a word to anybody?'

'Type,' said Smut cautiously, 'is one of those four-letter words you have to be careful with. Fair enough, in the normal course you'd say they're not. In an abnormal situation—'

'A break-in,' interrupted Mossop, 'by an armed mob? All four held hostage? Where are the signs of disturbance?'

'The gang cleaned up before leaving,' suggested Smut.

'Thanks. Try another.'

'They tricked them into going.'

'More promising. How?' The three of them had drifted back into the foyer.

'One at a time. Played one off against the other.'

'What for?'

Smut looked around. 'Any cash on the premises?'

35

'Don't know, do we? Might have been. There's a wall-safe behind that counter, no sign of it being tampered with. We'll get it looked at. For the moment—'

Somewhere a door opened noisily. The tramping of boots preluded the arrival from the lounge of Sergeant Willis, fronds of straw clinging to his uniform.

'Outbuildings all searched, sir. Not a sausage.'

'Questioned everyone?'

'I think so, sir. I think so.' Willis peered into his notebook. 'Nobody either side remembers hearing anything. Nor noticing anything: no movement, that is, from about ten onwards—'

'How about before then?'

'The girl, Maisie, as you know she was seen arriving. Likewise Miss—'

At a gesture from Mossop the sergeant retreated back into the lounge, where his superior joined him. Smut and Larkin looked at one another.

'Well, Jim?'

'Weird,' pronounced Larkin.

'That's the word,' Smut confirmed with enthusiasm. 'Weird Wonder in the West. Mystery at Miltham. Reckon it's too soon to alert PA?'

'Are you their local man?'

Smut drew himself up. 'I,' he said with dignity, 'am *the* local man. There is none other, that I wot of. Everything you read in the *Miltham Mail* stems from the single unimpeachable source. Now what I'm asking myself is, would a memo to London be premature or would I be justified . . . ?' He rolled his eyes.

'The police are investigating,' Larkin pointed out.

'Sure. Admittedly the riddle's only a few hours old at present, but you have to look at it in context. It's nine-forty, Jim. What do you think?'

'I think it's over a couple of hours to midnight.'

'Meaning I should wait?'

'You'll miss most of the editions,' Larkin conceded, 'but I can't help feeling—'

'The four of them might all stroll in any moment, having been en masse to see a flick at Launceston?'

'Something along those lines. It's too strange to be anything but easily explained. On the other hand—'

'The police,' reiterated Smut, 'are investigating. Wait while I just scribble something out.'

CHAPTER V

LARKIN AWOKE to the feeling that his head had been gently but continuously knocked against a wall for several hours during the night. Sitting up, he moaned. Sunlight battered at his eyes between half-drawn curtains. Hauling himself clear of the bed, he tottered to the washstand, ran cold water, hurled it against his temples.

The effect was zero.

Beyond the curtains the broad view was pleasing. Like an advertisement for somebody's coach tours, the countryside was drenched in the morning sun and bisected by a gently curving stream; speckling a distant hillside were numerous cows, already working time and a half to supply their multiple stomachs. Tree belts were abundant.

Closer to hand, the outlook was less expansive. Below his window a dirty cement roof intruded into a cinder and gravel yard which performed duty as the Royal's less than regal car park; he could see the boot of his MG and the rear half of the bulge-eyed family's Rover 2000, the remainder of both vehicles being hidden by the roof. Some yards to his right, a fire escape of rusting steel mounted the wall. In the exact centre of the cement roof, volumes of steam and a steady hissing rose from a ventilator.

At ground level, a dustbin lid smashed the silence. Larkin winced and closed the window.

The foyer was empty. Passing the rack on his way in to breakfast, he collected a *Daily Express* bearing his name in ink and unfolded it over the marmalade dish with his customary small thrill of anticipation, instantly doused. The family, as their table bore witness, had been and gone: he had the dining-room to himself. This condition persisted for a time. Eventually, as the climax to some scratching sounds, the screen yielded up the elderly waiter, who shook his way across with a dish of butter.

Larkin showed some teeth. 'A little behind time this morning.'

'Sorry to have kept you waiting, sir.'

'I meant myself. I overslept.'

The waiter fixed the butter scrupulously alongside the marmalade. 'That's forgivable, sir, on the first day. Splendid morning. A little brittle, perhaps.'

'Much too bright,' Larkin agreed, feeling more than brittle himself and wishing desperately that the old creature would silently bring him pungent coffee and silently depart. 'Pleasant for walking.'

'But you'll need to watch for showers. Do you have a map, sir, of the area? We provide a rather good one ourselves . . .'

Larkin got his breakfast and his solitude. The *Express* told him about a new oil refinery planned for the East Coast, and showed him a pop group grinning to fans at Heathrow. It told him nothing of events at the Stag Inn, Miltham. Even if PA had sent out Smut's story, this West Country edition would have missed it. Besides, he reminded himself, many a night news editor might have thought twice about a report of a country inn being deserted for six hours. Probably the Sandersons had now turned up. Moving on to the gossip page, he read that City tycoon Sir Peter Slabb was concerned about his daughter, £9 million heiress Melinda Slabb,

17, who was in Greece with an inappropriate young man who sold buckle belts from a boutique in Fulham. While he was pouring a third cup of coffee and reading what Sir Peter's estranged third wife in Sardinia had to say, Irene entered the dining-room with spring flowers which she proceeded to arrange in vases on window ledges.

'Hullo,' she greeted him. 'Found your paper, then?'

'Newsman's instinct,' he smiled.

Picking up the vase she was filling, she moved closer. 'What does your instinct tell you about the Stag affair?'

'That it's probably resolved itself. Heard anything?'

'Police are still there,' she said, frowning over her task. 'Hilda Cotteridge's sister is quite distraught, apparently.'

He laid aside the *Express*. 'There's no sign—?'

'None whatever. Smut will be in soon, he's been talking to Inspector Mossop and phoning London again. He said he wanted to see you.'

Larkin felt slight dismay.

'I'll be leaving soon on a hike. If he doesn't catch me, perhaps you'd tell him—'

'Tell him yourself,' said Smut, marching in purposefully. He sat at Larkin's table. 'Any of this coffee spare?' Larkin shoved it across. 'Hike, did you say? You can't be serious. With the yarn of the year stewing under your nostrils?'

Larkin gave him a gentle look. 'The reason I'm here, Smut, in the midst of a cold April, is supposed to be recuperation. I promised my pregnant wife I'd relax for a week and return in a fit state to assist her in becoming a mother in due course. I promised my partner not to take a ballpoint out of my pocket for seven days. I promised myself I'd keep my promises. You're advocating I abandon them?'

'Take no notice, Mr Larkin,' urged Irene.

'You stay out of this, sweetheart. You don't know Jim as I do. What he thrives on is toil, not torpor. Anyway I'm not asking him to flog his guts. I merely thought—'

'Stop merely thinking, then. Mr Larkin's on holiday.'

'Sure, sure.' Smut glanced slyly across Larkin's cup. 'All booked in, wasn't he, at the cosy old Stag? The Ghost Inn. Or was he? Here's the enigma. Did famous crime expert James Larkin slip up over his reservation? Or did he in his inimitable style happen upon a conundrum that's baffling top brains in the county constabulary? Detectives asking the question—'

'You don't ensnare me that way,' Larkin informed him.

'I don't? I don't.' Smut looked up lugubriously at his sister-in-law. 'Talk about waste. This is right up Jim's street.'

'No. The street is yours.'

'I still feel you're missing out. Okay: go for your walk and think about it. Suppose you get back this evening and the mystery's thickened?'

'Then,' said Larkin, rising from the table, 'I shall expect to hear all about it over a quiet pint in the bar.'

He investigated his packed lunch while sitting on his plastic mac on a grassed bank of the stream, which he had been studying for signs of pollution.

During the morning he had covered an estimated six miles, and some of it had been rough. The challenge of stiles, hillside tracks, ditches and gates had cleared his mind very satisfactorily of less immediate matters, implanted a healthy ache or two into his limbs, and sharpened his appetite. He was, he thought, unlikely to be disturbed here. In the course of his walk he had passed two human souls: a farmer who had grunted, vaulted a post and vanished behind hawthorn, and a woman motionless on a road verge, presumably waiting for transport. Her attire for a gusty April morning had comprised a thin pink cardigan and a black skirt, but she had seemed unaffected by the cold, although the sun had long since abdicated in favour of cumulus. Town dwellers, Larkin told himself, wore too much. He sighed and sampled a biscuit.

The stream looked clear, untroubled. No yellowed foam at the edges; no turgid bubbles on its surface. Perhaps the fish had grown too numerous and killed themselves off. He had heard that this could happen. No doubt it was easier to blame the plastics factory. More fulfilling: a tilt at modern trends. Reflecting on the ecological dilemma, he became aware of a sound behind him to his left. Between a shuffle and a drag.

Under his breath he sighed again. Lifting his head, he peered above the high grass that encircled him.

A figure was limping down the incline from the lane towards the water. He watched it with irritation. There was miles of the stream to choose from. Why here? Why ten yards from him, to stand on the bank and survey the current?

It was the woman he had seen previously, waiting on the verge. She was using the morning well. A vigil for a non-existent bus, followed by an interruption of someone's lunch-hour. Larkin was working himself to a fury. Mindful of his role—pipe-smoking English off-duty literary dilettante—he forced a mental smile, breathed determinedly, relaxed his hands. With a

42

synthetized indulgence he studied the side view of her, wondering why the buttons of her cardigan were undone so that it flapped in the breeze.

He further wondered why she was now removing the cardigan. Perhaps she had come to wash it. Could it be that the stream was after all dense with detergent? She seemed a tidy person. Folding the cardigan with care, she placed it on the grass behind her. She turned to face the water again.

Without hesitation she leapt.

Larkin was already on his feet. As she jumped he was running, and as her floundering body surfaced at the centre of the backwater pool he was wrenching off his sheepskin jacket and plunging in legs first beside her.

He went under and drifted up, all breath exploded out of him by the icy impact. When he had managed to gulp some back he made a grab.

She struggled feebly. Trying to touch bottom, he found that the pool was deep. His clothing dragged him down. Kicking with both feet, he got his face above surface, heaved air into his lungs. A flailing arm struck his face. Grasping it, he got behind her, tried to turn her on her back.

Now she was panicking violently. Her threshing weight descended on him, driving him under once more. This time he had some breath to hold. In addition his right foot touched bottom and he obtained a kick-start from a boulder. He surfaced beside her.

Burdened by moisture in the sleeve of his sweater, he raised an arm from the water and tried to measure his aim. Because of her convolutions it was impossible. The blow, when it landed, took her on the jawbone: she gave a gasping yelp and became rigid. Thankfully he worked himself into position, supported her head, towed her backwards.

At the pool's edge the next problem arose in the shape of a high and overhanging bank. He was near the end of his strength. Taking her along to the reef of rocks that formed the downstream limit of the backwater, he reached with his left hand, found a projection. With its help he elevated the upper half of her on to a slab, held her there while he struggled up himself, obscurely puzzled by the iron weights that had somehow come to be hung from each of his limbs. Kneeling on the slab, he heaved her further.

She neither helped nor resisted. Her body was slack, a dead weight. He paused to cough.

As soon as possible he began work on her where she lay. For a while it seemed useless. He persevered; presently she started to choke.

'It's Hilda Cotteridge all right,' Smut reported, 'and she's still with us, thanks to yourself. Beyond that she's being no help.'

'How so?' Advancing into his second brandy, Larkin dragged the bedroom chair closer to the electric bar. 'Is she refusing to talk?'

'More like inability than reluctance. Total amnesia, the quack thinks.'

'Inconvenient.'

'That's not what Mossop said. He used a word of four letters, not five syllables.'

'What's he doing about it?'

'Letting her rest, in the hope she'll recall something. A detective, as we professionals say, is at her bedside. Feel as though you might pull through?'

'If I don't,' said Larkin, setting down the tumbler,

'it won't be for lack of spiritous antidote. I must have practically de-stocked the hotel bar.'

'Knowing the Royal,' Smut said thoughtfully, 'you could well be right. They've a lousy cellar. Ahem. I've come, you see, complete with notepad and felt-tip. So when you're ready, Jim lad . . .'

Larkin extruded a groan.

'Not the full exclusive story? The *Miltham Mail* isn't out till Friday—'

'Who said anything about the *Mail?* London EC4 is waiting agog and aghast for my next flash, as the actor said to the magistrate. Look here.'

Producing with a flourish a copy of that morning's *Express*, Smut passed it across. Down-page on the front was a headline: *Phantom Inn Riddle.* Larkin read the few lines beneath and glanced up.

'There was nothing in mine about it.'

'Final edition, old son. Got it from Launceston at midday. They shoved *Envoy in Kidnap Drama* on to page nine to make room for that. What did I say? The media will love this. Give 'em a straight choice between fact and guesswork and see what wins, every time. So can we have the—' Smut paused to peer at the ceiling. 'What's overhead, a bunch of giraffes?'

'Either some leaden-footed guests,' Larkin said resignedly, 'or a resident staff member with a Great Dane. I may ask for a change of room. To return to the issue at hand, while conceding the news value of the situation into which I appear to have strayed, can it really be essential for my name to be appended to the narrative for the purposes of—'

'Not if you talk in extended prose couplets, no. Just answer a straight line of questioning. Did she say anything after you'd dragged her out?'

'She was too busy spluttering. We both were.'

'Not a damn thing?'

Larkin thought about it.

'She moaned once or twice while I was carrying her up to the lane, but the van driver who picked us up was somewhat too vocal to allow competition. She uttered no words at all.'

'I only wondered,' said Smut, looking disappointed, 'whether the amnesia came on after the cops got to her, and not before. You know. In the shock of the moment, people sometimes blurt things out.'

'Well, she didn't. Not in my hearing, anyhow.'

'No blurt. Maybe her sister can jog the embers.'

'How old is she?' asked Larkin.

'The sister, Mrs Thorpe? Must be sixty-odd. They've lived—'

'No, Hilda.'

'Late fifties. They've had this cottage out on the Pettersley road for quite a while. Irene would tell you, her parents know them.'

'They live there alone?'

'I believe Mrs Thorpe's husband fell under a tractor shortly after Suez. Since then—Look,' said Smut warmly, 'who's meant to be answering the questions around here?'

Larkin poured him a measure of brandy and handed it over. 'Smut, may I crave a boon? Keep my name out of it.'

'You don't want Bunty bothered?'

'You've hit it.'

'For you, Jim, I'll stifle my pen. "A holidaymaker"— how's that?'

'Fine. What else were you going to ask me?'

'You've put it out of my head.'

'Sorry. In that case, answer me another. How long has Hilda worked at the Stag?'

Smut drank his brandy, rose and walked to the door.

'I'll send Irene up. She's the one who's clued up on all the local—'

'I'm warm now,' said Larkin, reaching for a sweater. 'I'll come down and make it a desk inquiry.'

'She'll enjoy that.' Smut watched him quizzically from the door. 'You wouldn't be getting interested in this story, by any chance?' He was gone before Larkin could reply.

CHAPTER VI

'I'VE ALWAYS FELT vaguely sorry for her,' said Irene, taking her eyes from the road to look into Larkin's face. 'Why, I couldn't tell you. I suppose it's partly her being an old maid, but there's more to it than that. I can't explain. I'm just not surprised that she tried to commit suicide, that's all.'

'Interesting,' he said, wishing it were more interesting. 'She and her sister are fairly close, I imagine?'

'They're all they've each got,' Irene said after a pause.

'Does Hilda have to work at the Stag?'

'Financially, you mean? I really don't know. I expect she liked it—likes it. She's been there years.'

'As long as the Sandersons?'

'Longer than that. She was with the previous owners, the Barretts. They sold out in the late fifties. So it must have become a way of life to her. Are you sure you feel all right to be out?'

'I only took a ducking,' he said, amused. 'I've dried off. As long as I'm not keeping you from your duties.'

'Heavens no. It's the slack time of the afternoon. Michael will stand in for me. The boss's son,' she added.

Taking the car through a bend, he caught her with the smile that transfigured her face. She said pensively, 'There aren't many hectic times these days. Not since the fishing collapsed.'

'I gather you've been badly hit.'

'You want an entire floor to yourself, you can have it.'

'I don't ask for a floor,' he remarked, steering left at her direction, 'but I did mean to ask if I might swop rooms. Someone above me is a little less than feather-footed.'

She sounded puzzled. 'There's no one above you.'

'Not the family of three who arrived when I did? I thought it might be them.'

'They've moved on. The floor above you . . . I'll ask Mr Potter. There's the clinic,' she said, pointing. 'Park in front of the entrance. You think you'll find Mrs Thorpe here? She may have gone home.'

'From what I've heard about her,' said Larkin, 'I doubt it.'

Walking beside him to the door, Irene said, 'Smut will be furious that you came here without him.'

'I cleared it with him,' Larkin assured her. 'He's watching the Stag end of things and sending over frenzied stories to PA. We'll liaise this evening.'

'You said you weren't getting involved.'

'That's right,' he agreed. 'So I did.'

Inside, they were directed upstairs to a square landing. Sergeant Willis loomed from a door to intercept.

'Miss Cotteridge,' he informed them, having identified Larkin, 'can't see anyone for the—'

'It's her sister I wanted to talk to. Is she here?'

'Oh, Mrs Thorpe's here. Try keeping her away. You'll find her in there—' Willis pointed—'swigging tea.'

'No progress with Hilda?'

The sergeant swung his head. 'Just lies there, staring at the ceiling. Sort of fixed look in her eyes. Creepy.'

'Can't she talk?'

49   D

'I don't know if she can't, but she won't. Not to her sister, not to anybody.'

Mrs Thorpe was alone in a small antiseptic kitchen, nursing a teacup. A copy of *Woman's Realm* lay unopened on her knees. At sight of Irene her eyes widened.

'Hullo, dear. They didn't tell me—'

'I've brought Mr Larkin to see you, Mrs Thorpe.'

'Mr . . . ?' She gazed up at him without recognition.

'He rescued your sister.'

'Oh. Oh, do forgive me.' Impulsively she took his hand. 'I owe you such a lot. We do, I mean, Hilda and I. More than I can say. I hardly . . . I just don't know what made her do such a thing.'

'There'd been no signs?' Larkin asked.

'Signs?' Mrs Thorpe looked vacant. Her head shook. 'She left yesterday morning, just as she always did—'

'But before then. In the past few weeks.'

'I don't quite follow,' said Mrs Thorpe.

Larkin said patiently, 'Your sister hadn't appeared worried or preoccupied? Seemed to have nothing on her mind?'

Mrs Thorpe held her head.

'First the police . . . I've told them, she's been exactly the same as always—'

'She's a quiet one, your sister,' put in Irene.

'That's it, dear. A quiet person. Never very much to say for herself.'

'So if something was bothering her,' Larkin suggested, 'you perhaps wouldn't have known?'

She bristled immediately. 'I know all there is to know about Hilda. All her moods.'

'Of course,' he said placatingly. 'So yesterday she left at the usual time—'

'Stayed away the day and the night, and the next I

50

hear, she's been pulled out of the . . .' Plucking at a handkerchief, Mrs Thorpe put it to her eyes. They waited uncomfortably.

When she had stowed the handkerchief, Larkin said, 'You know, of course, about the others missing from the Stag? The police are looking into it. We're all wondering: could your sister have seen something? Which drove her to this?'

Mrs Thorpe considered the question with more control.

'I don't know,' she said at last. 'What could it have been?'

Sergeant Willis spoke gruffly from the doorway. 'Mrs Thorpe, she's moving her head. Like to have another try?'

Larkin and Irene waited on the landing until the sergeant re-emerged to report that still there was nothing to be had from Miss Cotteridge and that her sister was staying with her. Returning in silence to the car, they drove back towards the town.

Irene said, 'That didn't get us far, did it?'

'I wonder,' he replied obliquely, 'how far the police have got.'

'Scratching around,' said Smut, taking a deep and satisfying draught of best bitter. 'A nibble here, a pawing motion there. Candidly, they've no idea how to set about this. It's not conforming to the rules.'

'Rules?'

'The formula. They can't decide whether they're dealing with crime, accident, or an act of God. Mossop keeps prowling purposefully in and around the Stag, looking for something that might give off a smell like a clue. But a clue to what?'

'One sympathizes.' Larkin glanced around the Royal's bar. 'What's the feeling about it in the town?'

'Gleeful anticipation,' Smut answered promptly. 'Elements of the populace have been hanging about the place all day, hoping for something to tell their grandchildren in years to come.'

'Were they disappointed?'

'Unless they got a lift out of watching policemen striding through doorways and peering into dustbins. There was one moment of high drama when Maisie's aunt arrived back at the scene, but it died.'

'What was she there for?'

'To identify something of Maisie's—a knitted jacket. Found on a chest of drawers in one of the bedrooms.'

'Significant?'

'Well, there seems to be general agreement that part of Maisie's duties would be to help clean the rooms. And according to her aunt she gets hot very quickly. Her circulation,' said Smut reprovingly. 'So what could be more natural than for her to take off a thing like that while she was dusting, or whatever.'

'But it does indicate,' said Larkin, 'that on a coldish April day she left the inn without either jacket or coat.'

'And that's not all. Mrs Sanderson was in the habit of slipping on an old casual tweed coat with a fur collar whenever she went outside: it's well known. The coat's still hanging in the porch. And her husband's leather zip-up jacket with his wallet inside is on a hook in the annexe living-room.'

'Therefore if they went out, it was with the intention of being no more than a minute or two.'

'Looks that way.' Producing a notepad, Smut flicked through the pages, whistling softly into them.

'What are the Sandersons like?'

Smut glanced up. 'Nice couple. You'd like them. She's small and kind of fluffy, not silly but soft-looking: pretty efficient. Mousy hair, not much of a figure. He's not a lot bigger, but craggy, sort of officer presence. I believe he's an ex-tank commander.'

'And they were liked in the town? Are, I mean.'

'Sure, yes, I think so. You'll have to check by asking around.'

'I might,' corrected Larkin, 'if I were chasing up the story.'

'Climb off it, Jim. You're in it up to your shaggy eyebrows.'

'What makes you think so?'

'The strange light in your pupils. The fact you've not checked out and fled to five-star luxury at Plymouth. The fact you've got involved. The fact—'

'Excuse me.' Larkin rose. 'I've a call to make.'

Bunty answered instantly. She sounded agitated.

'Love, what are you doing across there?'

'I? What do you mean?'

'All this phantom inn stuff we're reading about. Stag Inn, Miltham—that is your dump, isn't it?'

'Yes, but I'm not—'

'Did they see you coming and clear off?'

'You may well have something. I'll put it to the fuzz. But I'm not—'

'What are you doing, cooking your own meals?'

'I'm staying at the Royal,' he said rapidly. 'The rival joint down the road. But I'm not *doing* anything. I'm here on holiday, I've told them—'

'Who?'

'Police, hotel people, Smut . . . you remember Smut from the *Review*? He's here, editing the local sheet. He sends his love.'

53

'Huh,' said Bunty. 'Don't let him talk you into anything.'

'Nobody will. Have the papers made a lot of it?'

'The evenings picked it up. Splash headlines inside. You'll have half Fleet Street there with you before you know it.'

'Blast Smut,' said Larkin, trying to sound cross.

'Why don't you try somewhere else?'

'If things get frantic I shall. But it's fine so far. Had a nice walk this morning.'

'What did you do this afternoon?'

'Er . . . rested, mostly. I went for a dip and it took it out of me.'

'You went for a *what*?'

'A swim. In a local pool. Bit cold.'

'You must be potty. Feel better for it?'

'Wider awake. How's everything?'

There was a pause. 'Aunt Dodie's crushing me with attention,' Bunty said suspiciously, 'but don't change the subject. Promise you won't *do* anything. Don't work.'

'The mere idea—'

'Have another walk tomorrow. Stay clear of the town till dinner. If anybody—'

The pips went. 'No more change,' he told the receiver. ''Bye now. Don't you do anything either.'

Holding the instrument, Larkin stared reflectively through to the bar where Smut was in conversation with Michael Potter, the proprietor's son. On impulse he put through a reversed-charge call to his partner's home in Islington.

'Alan? Sorry to disturb you. I just wanted—'

'I wouldn't have believed it,' said Feldham's lugubrious boom. 'I can hardly credit it now.'

'What?'

'What, queries he.' Feldham hissed, made tutting sounds into the mouthpiece. 'After weeks of threat and persuasion, we contrive to get you packed off for a rural tonic and what befalls? You damn well stroll into the middle of an updated *Mary Celeste*. What are you, some kind of catalyst? Keep your nose out, Jim, leave it to others.'

'Who said I wasn't? An ex-colleague of mine is doing all the slog. My stately role is merely to take impressions: there might be a chance to write the definitive account later. You can't deny me that. But what I want you to do—'

'No.'

'It's nothing at all. Just help me convince Bunty I'm keeping right out of it. If she asks you—'

'I can't lie, Jim, you know I can't.'

'There's nothing simpler. Tell her, if she calls, that as far as you know I'm pursuing my own devices. Which is absolutely the truth. Now I'm ringing off, I've some holidaying to do.'

'Tomorrow morning,' said his partner, 'I'm booking you a June cruise to the Greek islands. Once on board a ship—'

'See you next week,' said Larkin, 'and don't chafe.'

He hung up and returned to the bar.

'Jim,' said Smut, 'I don't believe you've met Mike Potter.'

'At a distance,' said Larkin, accepting a virile handshake across the tankards, 'and I've talked to your father. He was telling me about the blow to your trade here.'

'We mustn't exaggerate its effect,' said the younger Potter in a clear confident voice. 'One can't base one's

55

livelihood on a single factor. One has to work up alternatives. You'd know that, Mr Larkin, as a literary man.'

'You're no doubt right.' Larkin kept the dislike out of his voice. 'What alternatives do you have in mind?'

The younger man waved an arm. 'Plenty of motorists about.'

'But they don't come this way,' said Smut.

Michael smiled. 'They will. If the place gets known.'

'We've made a fair start on that,' Smut remarked.

'Better even than you may know,' said Larkin. 'I've just been speaking to Bunty. She says the London evenings have splashed the Stag affair.'

He observed a fleeting gleam in Michael's eyes. The younger Potter took an elegant taste of the gin and tonic he was holding. 'Does that mean the national Press are latching on?'

'They don't need a lot of persuasion,' said Larkin coolly.

'Good story, isn't it?'

'Depends where you're standing,' said Smut, filling in the interval. 'Hilda Cotteridge may not think so.'

'No, rough on her, of course. Odd business.'

'Any theories, Mr Potter?' asked Larkin with courtesy.

'Me? I help run a hotel, Mr Larkin, not an inquiry agency. I'm as stumped as the next man.'

'And worried?' suggested Smut.

'Worried? Why should I be?'

'For the Sandersons; and Maisie.'

'Ah. Naturally. I thought you meant—'

'You thought I meant, suppose something similar happened here at the Royal?'

Michael exposed some gleaming teeth.

'I didn't really imagine you meant that,' he said carelessly. 'Can I recharge your glasses, gentlemen?'

At ten o'clock Larkin excused himself and went upstairs. Fatigue from the day had begun to weigh upon him like heavily-saturated and suffocating cloth. Reaching the top of the staircase, he paused with a hand on the banister.

Ahead of him at the farther end of the broad landing shuffled the elderly waiter, carrying a tray. Passing through a curtained archway, he opened a door, turned the tray sideways and eased it through. The door shut behind him on a spring.

Eyeing it meditatively, Larkin let himself into his own room, reclosing the door but leaving it unlocked. He stood just inside, listening.

Thumping sounds became audible above. Then for a time there was nothing.

A faint 'clump' came to him. After a space this was followed by a laborious shuffling outside. When it had passed, he pulled the door ajar. The waiter, puffing to himself, was waiting in a weary attitude at the lift doors, holding the empty tray at his side.

CHAPTER VII

'SEEN THE PIECE in the *Mirror*?' asked Irene as Larkin emerged from breakfast. 'They've really gone to town.'

A four-column spread in a bold face on page two met Larkin's inspection. *Maid in Plunge Drama Sets New Riddle in Ghost Inn Probe* headed the account, assembled with some skill from Smut's notes via the Press Association: Larkin gave it high marks. 'Double-column only in the *Express*,' he said, showing it to her, 'but front-page to compensate. Indications are that Miltham's going to be much in the spotlight before long.'

'That'll make a change.' She stared at the print.

'Smut's struck it rich this time.'

'Looks like it. Oh, Mr Larkin, I've got your clothes here.' Diving behind the desk, she came up with a neat parcel. 'All dried out and pressed for you.'

'That is kind. Can I ask another favour?'

'Yes, what is it?'

'Call me Jim.'

The colour of her thin face heightened. 'Fine, okay. It's silly to be formal when you know Smut, and he's my brother-in-law—'

'And I'm the solitary guest . . . for the moment. Which reminds me, did you by any chance ask Mr Potter about what I said, you know, about the room?'

'No, I forgot. I'm sorry. I'll mention it today. Were you disturbed again?'

'Nothing to speak of. The odd thump, that's all, from the floor above. I wouldn't bother, but if other rooms are available . . .'

She screwed up her eyes. 'I can't understand it really. There shouldn't be—Oh look, here he comes. And doesn't he look pleased with himself?'

Smut entered with a swagger.

'We'll be rich together yet, sweetheart,' he informed Irene. 'Your large sister gave me a smacking kiss as a send-off this morning, which must mean something, if it's only goodbye.' His face fell suddenly. 'But it can't last. Can it, Jim?'

'Not with this amount of Fleet Street fascination.' Larkin showed him the papers.

'Seen that one. And that. What about the *Telegraph*?' Silently Irene handed him a copy. '*Mary Celeste Mystery on Dry Land*. Hey, that's not bad. It's right, isn't it? Everything shipshape, nothing out of place, crew vanished . . . Why didn't it occur to me?'

'Except,' Larkin pointed out, 'that one of the crew has reappeared.'

'True. But mute. Hushed by horror.' Smut rolled his eyes at his sister-in-law; the dolour dropped back. 'I've had it though. The nationals will be sending down any moment.'

'You've had a good run,' Larkin consoled him.

Irene looked indignant. 'Is this all you can think about, your linage payments? What about those poor people along there?'

'Along there,' Smut assured her, 'is just where they're not. Fuzz on the doors still, and no news.'

'No leads at all?'

'If there are, Mossop's hugging 'em to himself. Not a syllable out of the Cotteridge dame, apparently. All that happened yesterday was, some relative of the Sandersons got in touch to say she'd heard nothing from them but had been expecting to . . .'

'Madge Somebody?' murmured Larkin.

Smut looked startled. 'She called herself Madge Pearson. How'd you know that?'

Larkin explained about the half-completed letter he had seen in the Sandersons' living-room. Smut placed a solemn hand on his shoulder.

'Jim lad, you've lost none of your touch. Now listen. Will you do something for me this morning?'

'Tell me what it is,' said Larkin, 'and in deference to past friendship I'll consider it before turning you down.'

The cottage of Maisie's aunt was set back from the meaner end of the main street, wedged between a florist's and a bakery. It was approached by a strip of garden swamped by matted grass and nettles. The roof-thatch was under attack by alopecia.

'Not exactly Mon Repos, as you can see,' said Smut, staring at it through the windscreen of Larkin's car. 'Suits her, I always think. Kind of thin, compressed look about it. No wonder we hate each other.'

'What caused the vendetta?'

'Maisie got into some trouble last year. Aiding and abetting a couple of lads to take and drive away a car. She got an absolute discharge, but of course I had an immediate visit from Auntie: could I keep Maisie's name out of the paper? She's never believed I couldn't have if I'd wanted. So as far as I'm concerned, it's been the big freeze ever since.'

'She's probably agin all newspapermen.'

'Go in there, Jim, like a pal. Melt her down. It's our last chance, I'm convinced, before the competition gets keen.'

'What do I use on her, the stern unrelenting gaze of authority or the high-powered charm?'

'Try one,' said Smut anxiously, 'and if it flops, try the other.'

'You can bathe my bruises afterwards.' Climbing out, Larkin walked across to the gate. It fell flat at his touch. Propping it up again, he followed the overgrown path to the door and rapped. A curtain stirred at a side window.

Presently, without having noticed the opening of the door, he found himself looking at her. Her mouth was almost non-existent. He said without delay, 'I must have a word with you, please, Mrs Charles,' and placed a foot on the doorstep.

She fell back, like a second rickety gate. He followed her into what was indisputably a parlour, washed in pale lilac, with mud-brown woodwork. The effect was so appalling that he wanted to back out again. Standing erect in the centre of the room—the only portion not smothered by furniture—he regarded her with bland officialdom.

'It's about Maisie. Sit down, please, Mrs Charles.'

She obeyed. 'I told the other gentleman—'

'Yes, and I want you to tell me. I represent the Press, which is vitally concerned in this matter,' said Larkin, keeping faith with his conscience. 'Anything you say could be important. Maisie's general behaviour, for example, in the past few days or weeks.'

'Keeping out of trouble, she was. Had her fill of courtrooms, she had, and so'd I.'

He said curtly, 'I'm sure you both had. But it's her demeanour I want to hear about. Did she seem excited, upset? Frightened, even?'

'What she got to be frightened of?'

'I'm asking you.'

Mrs Charles shook her head, keeping her mouth visible in readiness for the next question. She was still wearing the greenish beret.

'Was she—is she secretive?' He tried again. 'Does she keep things from you?'

'She's a girl,' said her aunt scornfully.

He said persuasively, 'Maisie's already had a little trouble with the law. I understand she helped drive away a car. Does she like cars?'

'Led into it, she was.'

'Very likely. But if she hankers to drive . . . She passed her driving test, I believe?'

Mrs Charles nodded briefly. He gazed thoughtfully at the stonework face confronting him, and drew a breath. 'Did—does Maisie like living here with you?'

She stared flintily into his left hip. More gently he said, 'She wasn't too happy, perhaps?'

'Missed her mum an' dad.' The words came out of her as though they had formed themselves.

'They died when she was young?'

'Broke up. Never heard no more of either of 'em.'

'So you took Maisie in. Why was that?'

'I'm her dad's sister, en't I? Wasn't no one else.'

'Were you glad to do it?'

She shrugged. 'Never thought much about it.'

'I've not met Maisie,' he said after an interval. 'Is she a good-looking girl—pretty?'

She looked away at a plate-strewn dresser. 'Best ask a few others.'

'Which others,' he inquired carefully, 'would that be?'

She turned back to face him. 'See here, mister. Maisie and me never got on, I don't pretend it. She's gone her own way. Come back here to sleep of nights, but she ate her food at the Stag an' she lived her own life an' that's the way it was.'

Larkin pondered.

'One would have thought, then, she'd have had her own room at the Stag and slept there.'

The idea seemed to outrage Mrs Charles, but not for conventional reasons. 'They've just the seven rooms. Couldn't give her one of them.'

'Why not?'

She looked at him pityingly. 'Cos o' visitors, of course.'

'But half the time there haven't been any.'

'But what if there was?' She regarded him with thin triumph.

He abandoned the point. 'You haven't by any chance a recent photo of Maisie?'

Her mouth took a dive. To his surprise, however, she rose and went to a drawer of the dresser. She came back with a print.

'This here's what the police didn't want. They took the others.'

Larkin examined the sulky-smiling face eyeing him from a frame of straight fair hair. A fringe narrowed the forehead, giving Maisie a gamin aspect. He said, 'She looks about sixteen here.'

'They had it taken at the Fete,' she replied indifferently.

'Who did?'

'Them running it. Bank Holiday Princess, she was.'

'May I take this with me?'

For less than a second she hesitated. 'You can take it if you want.'

'Thank you.' He tucked it away. 'I shan't intrude

63

more on your time, Mrs Charles. I hope you have some news soon.'

She made a slight movement of the shoulders. He went to the door and opened it. Before stepping outside he looked back. 'I may be wrong, but I have the feeling you'd like to have been proud of her.' She turned to face the dresser. Cursing himself, he trod the undergrowth to the gate.

The road from Miltham towards Launceston was a beauty. Arriving two days earlier, Larkin had been too weary to notice; this time he drove sedately, glancing to each side to take in the views.

Calling in for a lunchtime sandwich at a pub, he complimented the landlord on the scenery. His host, a wizened elderly man, mourned the departed fish. Larkin mentioned the plastics factory. The landlord said Ah, that was reckoned to be at the bottom of it, never mind what they said. Local feeling about it, Larkin conjectured, must run high. The landlord said Ah, them factory fellahs wasn't so popular.

'As a matter of fact,' said Larkin, 'I'm on my way to see it now.'

He received a look of dark suspicion. 'You from the Council or some such place?'

Hastily he denied the charge. 'I came here to do a spot of angling and found what had happened. So I thought I'd have a look at the culprit.'

'You'll not be the first.' The landlord shook his shrivelled head. 'Council officers, men from this commission and that inspectorate, they've all had a go. Nothing's done.'

'The factory hasn't improved its discharge arrangements?'

64

'If it has,' said the other bitterly, 'the fish haven't been told.'

Another four-mile drive took Larkin to the edge of the industrial area that had been created on the outskirts of the village of Pettersley, in the centre of which he had noted with amusement the branch office of the *Miltham Mail*: a dust-streaked window over a confectionary shop. There was nothing amusing about the industrial area. It grew like a thistle-patch out of a lawn. Diligent elimination brought him at length to the ribbed concrete encircling the premises of Pettersley Plastics and from there, on foot, to the glistening office of the company secretary, who was still at lunch.

'I'll wait,' Larkin said politely to the female assistant, a beak-nosed woman clad in defensive armour of belted suède jacket and trousers, although her need for such equipment was not apparent.

He waited forty minutes. Through a window of the outer office he could follow the erratic course of the stream, broader here, on its sluggish way to the brisker reaches around Miltham. To his layman's eye the water was of a normal hue. He was frowning in the direction of some machinery next to a weir when the assistant reappeared to say that Mr Cox would see him at once and to give him a hastening smile of such muzzle-velocity that he almost ducked. Mr Cox, secure at the far side of an enormous, shiny and completely nude desk, half-rose and leaned across with outstretched palm.

'Mr . . . Larkin? Something I can help you with?'

Larkin explained that he was investigating the departure of fish from the district. A look of fatigue overcame Mr Cox. For an article, Larkin added. Alarm added itself to the weariness. 'I've spoken

E

already,' Larkin told him brutally, 'to a number of locals, and got their side of it. Now, naturally, I'd like to obtain yours.'

Hunted, Mr Cox excused himself to make an internal phone call.

'Sir? I've a Mr ... Larkin with me, a journalist. He's doing a story on the fish controversy. I'm not quite clear on that ...' Covering the mouthpiece, he said, 'Anything to do with the *Miltham Mail*?'

'Nothing whatever,' Larkin said agreeably. 'I'm free-lance, working for the nationals.'

'National Press, sir. Yes. Well, it could do, at that. My view entirely. Quite. I'll do that.' Mr Cox disconnected. 'You're aware there have been stories already, in our local publication and elsewhere?'

Larkin said he was, but he felt they hadn't gone fully into the matter. Mr Cox nodded with some eagerness.

'The company's side of the story has generally finished up the worse for wear, I'm sorry to say. There was one particular version ... But I won't go into that.' Apprehensively he settled himself. 'Will you ask questions, or shall I simply recite our case?'

To prompting, he described the measures taken, the precautions, the checks, the installations, the filtering plants and the safety devices that in the company's view, in the view of every supervisor and pollution expert sent along to vet the arrangements, almost certainly ruled out any possibility of contamination from the factory's discharged waste. He enlarged on the additional work undertaken since the commencement of the outcry. He referred to the samples taken regularly from stream water for miles around, all triumphantly vindicating the company's assertion that fish could not only live in it if they wished, but should actually be shouldering each other aside to do so. Larkin, he said, could interview the managing director, the plant overseer or the chief engineer, or all three, separately or together, if he felt the urge. In addition, Larkin could be taken on a tour of inspection of the filtration and purification sections to see for himself. Declining the invitation, Larkin opted for a perusal of the plump file of complaints that had been compiled in the course of the factory's initial years of anxious operation.

'We're conscious of our responsibilities,' averred Mr Cox, handing it across, 'and, if I may say so, of our image. We don't want to offend people round here. We want to fit in, be accepted.' It was an age-old, plaintive cry from the heart. 'We've done all we're legally obliged to do, and a great deal more. I wish you could bring that home to everybody.'

Larkin went through the file with interest. He asked if he could take away one or two of the photographs of installations: Mr Cox implored him to take a handful. After that the correspondence seized his attention. There had been a lot of it.

One letter, typed on headed notepaper, held him for several minutes. He read it twice, memorizing its salient points. Watching, Mr Cox cleared his throat.

'You'll see that some of our critics have been more than a little . . . importunate.'

'They've kept at it,' Larkin agreed. 'This one interests me. Would you say it's typical of the general tone?'

'May I see?' Mr Cox frowned at it. 'Oh, this. Couched a bit extravagantly, we thought. I really don't see that we can be held accountable for a drop-off in the tourist trade. Stretching it too far. The local authority backed us up on that, you'll notice.'

Larkin passed back the file. 'At the same time, one can appreciate their concern.'

'Oh certainly. I trust we conveyed that in our reply.' Mr Cox studied the file again. 'Isn't this the place where there's just been that rather odd business . . . ?'

'It is indeed. Having no luck, is it, just lately?'

'Depends,' said the secretary meaningfully, 'what you mean by luck. I'm an accountant, Mr Larkin, and I'm also a believer in the logic of reaction. To a situation, that is. With the abuse we've had, you might not have blamed us for shutting down, trying elsewhere. But we didn't. We reacted positively. We met the objections, we did all this extra work, we diversified our precautionary measures and we've gained official sanction. It might do some of these people more good if, instead of writing us letters, they got down to diversifying their own activities.'

Larkin looked at him with a faint smile.

'That process,' he remarked, 'may already have got under way.'

CHAPTER VIII

HE ARRIVED back at the Royal at five-thirty. As a salve for his conscience, which was proving increasingly troublesome, he had taken a walk beside the stream on leaving the factory and had covered more ground than intended. He felt overtired now; empty rather than hungry. Giving him her quick smile, Irene reached for his room key.

'Any developments?' he asked, jerking his head Stag-wards.

'Not that I've heard. Smut looked in, said he'd see you before dinner.'

'Right. Rather a lot of cars at the back. Had a rush of visitors?'

'We're practically full,' she said on a note of amazement. 'They're all down from London.'

'Pressmen?'

She nodded. 'Several of the dailies, and one or two TV people. They've taken all the rooms. Jim, I'm sorry—it happened so fast I forgot all about switching you. There's just one poky little cubicle at the end of the—'

'Forget it. I'm fine where I am. What had Smut to say about it?'

'He's wearing his tragedy mask,' said Irene in a practical way. 'He knew it had to happen, but I think he was hoping for one more clear day. I suppose this means the media have really got the scent?'

'Baying on the trail,' Larkin said abstractedly. 'See you later.'

On the landing he walked into an acquaintance who worked on the *Globe*. 'Well, well,' he said. 'Managed to wangle a country trip, then.'

'Greetings, Jim. Didn't waste any time yourself, did you? What's this going to be, the unvarnished insight exclusive in three weeks' time in the supplements?' Drawing Larkin aside, Gavin Foster lowered his voice. 'Got anything on these people, old boy? The Sanderson pair, and especially this teenage chick. Ex-beauty queen, isn't she?'

'If you know that, you know as much as I do.'

'Come *on*, Jim. What harm in a spot of barter?'

'I've nothing to offer. Believe it or not, I'm here on holiday.'

Foster looked at him sadly. 'Of course you are. Did I tell you, I'm here on doctor's orders? Low alcohol pressure. Well, see you, Jim. *Should* you change your mind, I'm in room eleven.' He pointed significantly, gave Larkin another sorrowful survey and ambled away to the stairs.

Difficulties lay ahead, mused Larkin, closing and bolting his door.

An hour later he went down to the bar. It was full of very large men.

'Here's the chappie!' The chief crime reporter of the *Citizen*, a forty-year-old who looked sixty and behaved as though he were twenty, came forward to encircle Larkin with an arm thinly encased in man-made fibres. 'Have a noggin, Jim, and give.'

'Give what, Ian?'

'Can you beat it?' Ian Butler appealed to colleagues. 'Modesty sat well upon our hero . . . but enough's enough. Tell us what she said, Jim, when you dragged her out.'

'Not with you. Cider, thanks.'

'*Cider!*' Butler blinked, but recovered speedily and gave the order to Michael Potter. He breathed whisky into Larkin's right eye. 'We know it was you, Jim. They told us at the nick.'

'If it's Hilda Cotteridge you're talking about, I read that it was a holidaymaker who didn't give his name.'

'Fuzz say it was you. They don't get things like that wrong, old boy.'

'Then you'd better say so, hadn't you?'

'Not if it's a balls-up,' said Butler uneasily. He handed Larkin a pint of draught cider. 'You saying they've boobed?'

'I'm saying nothing,' smiled Larkin. 'Cheers.'

Butler studied him with deep suspicion, muttered and turned away. Other reporters, unknown to Larkin, threw him glances of passing interest and resumed their own discussions. He took his cider, gained under false pretences, to a padded bench in a corner beneath a black-oak beam hung with cut-out anglers and fish-baskets; from there he watched Michael serving at the bar. The man knew his job. His black curls and gleaming teeth remained constant as he whirled and darted, coping expertly with the sudden demand. Larkin took a thoughtful pull at the cider.

'You're not alone any more,' said a voice.

He looked up to find the senior of the Potters at his elbow.

'Far from it,' he agreed. 'This is the kind of influx you have to be ready for, I imagine, at any time?'

The proprietor smiled ruefully. 'Our preparations haven't been needed for an awfully long while. But tonight, I must say . . .' He glanced around the

71

animated room. 'One realizes, of course, it's just a flash in the pan.'

'Another's loss, your gain.'

'I'd sooner it wasn't like that.' Potter was silent for a moment. 'Ironic, really,' he resumed. 'For two years the Sandersons have been worst hit by the fishing slump—though of course we've all suffered. Now there's a sudden boom, they're not here to take advantage.'

'If they were, the boom wouldn't be.'

'Exactly. Life's very odd. I wish I knew what had become of them.' Potter stared at nothing.

'No progress today?' asked Larkin.

'The police don't say much. They seem to be poking around a bit haphazardly. Rumour abounds, of course.'

Larkin made a non-committal noise and drank cider.

'Where a young girl's involved,' said Potter, watching the tankard, 'I suppose that's inevitable.'

'A girl and a married couple,' Larkin said neutrally.

'Yes. But if you knew the Sandersons . . . They were like parents to Maisie. I'm not being naïve. They genuinely were.' Potter paused. 'Are, I should say.' He glanced quickly at Larkin's face and looked away.

'I spoke to Maisie's aunt this morning.'

'Yes?' The older man gave him a keener inspection and joined him on the bench. 'Might as well rest my limbs for a bit . . . Was she forthcoming?'

'In an inarticulate way,' said Larkin. 'I gained the impression that Maisie's been a disappointment to her.'

Potter seemed to consider this. At last he said, 'Excellent woman though she is, Mrs Charles never did get on with Maisie. I rather think she saw it as her duty to look after the girl, and perhaps resented it.'

'I see. You know Mrs Charles, then?'

'She's my tenant, as a matter of fact.'

'Really?'

'Yes, I own the cottage she's in. Between ourselves, she pays an absurdly low rent, but then it is in a bit of a state.'

'I expect she's glad to have it,' said Larkin. 'Have she and Maisie lived there long?'

'A few years,' said the other vaguely.

Larkin gave a sudden chuckle. 'Funny, in a way.'

'What is?'

'Maisie, a tenant of the owner of the Royal, going to work at the Stag.'

'I was happy about it,' said Potter good-humouredly. 'In fact it was I who got her the position. The Sandersons are perfectly good friends of mine.'

Larkin nodded. 'Most people seem to think well of them.'

'They run a very good house. The Stag has always—'

'But as people?'

'Very sincere,' said Potter on consideration. 'Friendly and kind. As I say, they treat Maisie like a daughter. Her little brush with the law last year—you heard about that?—made no difference whatever. They kept her on, held nothing against her.'

'And she gets on well with them?'

'Better than a natural daughter would, probably.'

Larkin gave another nod and set down his tankard. 'What about Hilda Cotteridge?'

Potter took his time answering. Finally he said, 'I can guess what brought her to do it.'

Catching Larkin's questioning glance, he added, 'The state of trade, I mean. The Stag's been her life, poor soul. She was afraid it would have to shut down.'

'Would she really take it so badly?'

'You'd need to know her background.' Potter stared at a knot of newsmen whose exchanges were becoming raucous. 'Like myself, she's lived in this region all her life and has a sort of fierce affection for it. Embodied in the Stag. She was in service there when I was . . . quite young. When the Sandersons took it over it was accepted without question that she soldiered on.'

'Full-time?'

'Well, this is the point. Up to a couple of years ago she was needed all day, every day. Then the rot set in. Both the Stag and ourselves got many fewer visitors, and I know the Sandersons were feeling the pinch . . .'

'They cut down her hours?'

'They were prepared to hang on, hoping things would improve—but in the meantime they asked Hilda to reduce her attendance to half-days.'

'And this worried her?'

'I'd say she took it very much to heart.' Seizing Larkin's tankard, Potter stood. 'Let me refill this for you.'

He steered a path to his son at the bar. Larkin stretched, took out his pipe, remembered dinner and regretfully stowed it again. Gavin Foster scowled at him from the edge of a group. Larkin answered with a row of teeth.

'So this could explain a lot.' Potter returned with more cider and a sherry for himself. 'Bookings at the Stag so far this year, I happen to know, were the worst ever. There's a real danger it'll have to close. The thought may have been too much for Hilda. Good health.'

Larkin poured some more unwanted cider into himself. 'You don't think,' he asked, 'the Sandersons could have suddenly lost heart, washed their hands of the place and gone off?'

'Leaving their clothes? His wallet? The car?' Potter shook his head with vigour. 'They'd have to have been mad. Besides—'

'There's Maisie.'

'Yes. And there'd be no point to it anyhow. If they'd decided to give up, they'd have sold, got what they could out of the place.'

'Getting back to Hilda,' said Larkin, 'how dependent is she on—'

He became aware that his host was looking restively past him. Glancing the same way, he saw Smut at the bar entrance. With an apology Potter scrambled up. 'Time's getting on. I must go and look after things in the kitchen.'

Carrying his sherry, he took a circuitous way out, by-passing Smut who was pursuing a direct line for the corner. On arrival he cast a critical glance at Larkin's cider, said 'Join you in a second,' and went off for a pint of bitter.

'Your worst fears,' observed Larkin at his return, 'have been realized.'

Smut stared glumly at the crowd. 'I only wonder they took so long.'

'What have you been up to?'

'Following the course of non-events. Was that the owner I saw you with?'

'Yes. We were discussing the *affaire* Stag when suddenly he remembered the joint.'

'Not the joint,' Smut said calmly. 'Me.'

'He's anti the *Mail*?'

'Cordially dislikes its editor. So far as I can make out,

he thinks I shoved my oar in to stop a romance between Irene and his Michael.'

Larkin lifted his eyebrows. 'And did you?'

Smut looked offended. 'What am I, the latest threat to Cupid? Irene can decide for herself, she usually does.'

'So where did he get the idea?'

'Well, I look in to see her a lot. Maybe he thought . . . I don't know. The fact is, Irene was never interested. She puts up with Mike all right, but that's as far as it goes.'

'Is Michael keen on her?'

'Not noticeably. To be frank, old Potter was only trying to use Irene, I imagine, to counter the threat of someone else who was making a play for Mike.'

'Who?'

Smut answered from the side of his mouth. 'Young Maisie, I believe. What you might call a tenant/landlord relationship.'

'I see,' said Larkin slowly. 'Potter senior didn't care for that?'

'The idea seemed to terrify him. I suppose he didn't regard her as Michael's type. I'm not sure Michael did himself. He never seemed to encourage Maisie.'

'And he seems to bear you no malice about Irene.'

'I don't think Mike even knew what was meant to be happening. Anyway Irene's hardly his mug of cocoa— he's probably got someone flashy in Launceston. Be that as it may,' said Smut with a flourish of his tankard, 'this explains the hasty exit of his dad, who's convinced I tried to thwart him.'

'Tell me about your day,' said Larkin presently.

'Yes, darling. Well, to put you briefly in the picture:

there's no picture. No sign of the missing three; not a bleat out of Hilda, who's been allowed home with her sister; and just about everyone in Main Street and points west has been ruthlessly quizzed, first by the Mossop gang and this afternoon by that shower . . .' Smut indicated the drinkers. 'With special emphasis on Maisie's aunt, who's now barricaded herself behind drawn curtains and locked doors and is not at home to callers. Prints of Maisie and the Sandersons are being handed out tomorrow.' Absorbing the last of his bitter, Smut sat back with a gasp and drew a sleeve across his face. 'How'd you make out, Jim?'

'One or two things of interest,' said Larkin, and told him.

Notwithstanding the enlistment of both Irene and Michael into the serving strength, dinner was an extended affair. The abrupt stresses imposed were taxing the Royal's creaking machinery. Gaps yawned between courses. In sharp contrast to his previous isolation, Larkin found himself sharing a table with Gavin Foster, a young reporter from the *Sun*, and a dimple-cheeked, medium-aged woman called Elaine Hurst with a sweet smile and an interior, as Larkin had guessed from her weekly column in the *Examiner*, baked to the density of granite. Foster made introductions.

'So you're the one,' exclaimed Elaine, 'who rescued this Hilda—'

'He denies it,' Foster said sourly.

'But the sergeant—'

'Got it wrong,' said Larkin, delivering a quarter-special to her left dimple.

'I don't think he could have done, you know.' She smiled back. Larkin felt the blast. 'There your name was, down in the incidents book, James Larkin, in black on white.'

'Turn it up, Jim,' counselled Foster.

He capitulated. 'In confidence, then, it was me. I was keeping it dark for the sake of my wife.'

'Your wife's Here With You?' Elaine asked in initial capitals.

'No.' Tiredly he explained the position.

'So you didn't want her to worry.' Elaine made a flank attack upon gammon steak. 'I do see that, Jim— but your secret's out, you know.'

'So it appears.'

'She'll be Proud Of You.' Daintily her teeth tore the gammon apart. 'We shan't embarrass you in any way. Shall we, boys?' Dimples prominent, she turned back to him. 'How is it you were so near to this Hilda What's-it when she tried it on?'

Larkin said smoothly, 'I was out for a walk.'

'What a healthy idea. And she just happened to choose the place where you were at the time?'

'There's an opening to it from the lane.'

'So I suppose,' she said consideringly, 'it was natural enough.' Delicately she speared a morsel. 'Did she gasp her thanks, or hurl abuse, or what?'

'She said nothing whatever.'

'Consistent, anyhow,' remarked Foster. 'I tried to get to her today. No joy.'

'Gone home, hasn't she?' The *Sun* reporter, who looked inexperienced, gazed anxiously around the table. 'They told me there's a police watch on her.'

'For my money,' said Elaine, ignoring him, 'it's local rumour that tells most in these cases.'

'Rumour,' repeated Foster.

'That's right, dear.' She devoted herself to her plate.

Foster lifted an eyebrow at Larkin, who raised two back. He was glad when the meal limped to an end, enabling him to undertake a lengthy programme of pipe-packing and igniting while one by one the others made off, Elaine last. She paused at Larkin's shoulder. 'The Sandersons,' she fluted, 'were such nice people. Everyone says so. What do you hear about them, Jim?'

'Much the same as you, Elaine.' He looked sideways and up at her; their eyes met. 'And one can only go, can't one, by what one hears?'

'Until events put in a word.' She dimpled and departed.

Larkin sat on. The old waiter quavered across and began gathering plates. Larkin said to him, 'I doubt if you expected anything like this?'

'Hard to know what to expect, sir, in the catering business.'

'Have to be ready for anything, I suppose,' Larkin said cheerfully. 'Shortages of food and tables; meals in rooms—'

'That's it, sir.' The waiter swept breadcrumbs into a dish with a cupped palm. 'Though that's a thing we've never provided at the Royal.'

'What is?'

'A room service of meals. We find that once you start it . . .' He waved a claw.

'Pity,' said Larkin. 'I was planning to ask for breakfast in bed. I thought I'd seen trays being taken to people's rooms.'

'I think you must be mistaken, sir. Of course, if someone became ill . . .'

'I'll have to dream up some painless disease.' Larkin rose, puffing at his pipe. 'You'll be wanting to get finished. Quite like old times, I imagine?'

79

The waiter raised his ravaged face and a smile spread across it.

'Good to have the bustle again,' he said softly.

Larkin paused at the reception desk. Waiting until she had repulsed the leering representative of a mass-circulation Sunday who wanted to know about the town's night-spots, he beckoned Irene to his end. 'If Smut looks in again, tell him I'll be back in an hour.'

'All right, Jim.' She eyed him with a straight face. 'Going swimming?'

'Fishing,' he told her, and went upstairs for his coat.

CHAPTER IX

OPENING THE CAR DOOR, he looked up at the Royal's rear elevation.

Through the gloom, he was able by tracing the line of the fire escape to pinpoint his window on the second floor: above it was the roof and a row of dormer windows. These he watched steadfastly for a while. Then he ducked into the MG and accelerated meditatively away.

Smut's directions had been clear, but he lost himself twice before finding the cul-de-sac he was looking for. The house was one of four in a depressingly new terrace. He pressed the illuminated bell-push and prepared his features. A light snapped on.

'Mrs Appleby?' he asked the blonde who revealed some of herself.

'Yes, and if you're another one from the papers—'

'No; I'm carrying out inquiries.'

Nothing disputable, he reflected, about that statement. She regarded him sullenly.

'Want me husband? He's having his supper.'

'I'll wait for him to finish, if you don't mind.' He gave her a smile, a full 22-carat Larkin super-special which rebounded from her dead-white face to smash uselessly over the floor. In silence she stood aside, allowing him to step past. The hall smelt of children and washing.

'You from the dairy?'

'No.'

At a nod, he went into a small front room peppered

with toys. A high-chair stood against a table. He tripped over a plastic tractor. Recovering, he turned. 'When your husband's got a moment—'

She had disappeared. He heard a door clump. Resting against the table, he resigned himself to a vigil.

Almost immediately the door clumped again. A thin young man strode in and with a flouncing movement closed the door.

'Who's it this time?'

Larkin said with sympathy, 'You've had many interruptions today . . .'

Appleby, whose lengthy auburn hair mantled deepset eyes established in a permanent frown, threw him a swift mirthless grimace.

'What's one extra? You the police again?'

'I've no connection with the police. I'm carrying out inquiries on behalf of Miss Cotteridge. Now I understand you're the chap who delivered milk to the Stag Inn on the morning the Sandersons vanished, and I'd like you to tell me—'

A sigh issued from the young man's chest.

'Mate, you can get this from the sergeant.'

'Not in your words, I can't. I'll be most grateful, Mr Appleby, if you'll sit down and try to relax and answer my questions. The answers could be very important.'

'Can't give you no answers.' Appleby lolled against the door and folded his arms.

'You gave the police some.'

'Mostly No. Did I see 'em when I called that morning? No. Did I hear anything? Not much. This is all I've been saying.'

'Then let's see,' smiled Larkin, 'if we can't give you the chance to elaborate. What I'm after is the infilling.

The supplementary detail that a chap like you can give me. You've been with the dairy some time?'

'Year.'

'And you always deliver to the Stag?'

'Most days.' Appleby elevated a forearm to scratch his chin.

'As well as to the Royal, I presume. The whole Main Street, in fact? How many pints to the Stag, as a rule?'

'Depends.' The young man shrugged. 'Off-season, maybe three or four. Can be ten or a dozen.'

'What do you call off-season?'

'The whole bloody year, mate.'

'But technically?'

'December to end of Feb.'

'How many pints did you leave that morning—the day they went missing?'

Appleby screwed up his eyes. 'Six.'

'By arrangement, of course. That was the number asked for the previous day?' Appleby nodded. 'By whom?'

'Mrs Sanderson.'

'You spoke to her? Where was that?'

'Back door to the kitchen.'

'She appeared quite normal?'

Appleby sucked in both cheeks to reflect. 'Seemed okay to me.'

'And she ordered six pints. Did she mention they had someone coming for a week?'

'Nope.'

'You spoke just now about the off-season. Did they— do they close the inn during those winter months?' Larkin added hurriedly, 'Do you happen to know?'

'Block off a few rooms, I reckon,' said his informant grudgingly. 'They keep open, though, case of any trade.'

'I see. To get back to this milk business: how do you deliver?'

'Huh?'

'By van,' Larkin said patiently, 'or handcart, or what?'

'Van.'

'At the Stag, you drive through the side entrance to the enclosed yard at the back?'

'Right,' said Appleby restively.

'Just a few more questions. Where do you leave the bottles?'

'Kitchen door.'

'Outside?'

'Just inside.'

'Normally you'd open the door to do that?'

'If it's shut.'

'Was it on this occasion? The day they vanished?'

Appleby pondered again. 'Can't remember.'

'At all events, you saw and heard nobody?'

The young man shook his head.

Larkin awarded him the friendliest of smiles. 'I'd have thought,' he said kindly, 'if you recalled delivering six pints and hearing or seeing nothing, you'd have remembered if the door was shut.'

'Yes, well I don't.'

'Right you are. I'm nearly through. What type of van do you have—the enclosed sort or an open float?'

Appleby straightened, tugged open the door and held it.

'Look, mister. I'm fair whacked, right? Been on the round, one of the kids is ill, and me wife's starting to get at me. If you want to know what vans we use, you look around you, mate. You'll see one pass sooner or later.' Head cocked in a challenge, he pulled the door wide.

'I can take a hint,' said Larkin, ambling through. 'You've been extremely patient and helpful. I'm sorry about your child. Nothing serious I hope?'

'Asthma. She wants a holiday.'

'Hm. Any hopes?'

Appleby shrugged. 'Depends.'

Himself opening the front door, Larkin stepped into the night. 'Thanks again,' he said, 'and if you should happen to remember—'

'Okay, mate.' The door closed in his face.

He felt tired. Desperately, unbelievably somnolent. After a quick word with Smut he excused himself, took the lift to his room and bolted himself in. He undressed in a stupor. Throwing his trousers on to the chair, watching them slip to the floor and doing nothing about it, he wondered for the first time whether Feldham had been right about him. 'You're not just stale, Jim, you're sprouting mildew. If you don't pause now, you'll halt later.' He had laughed at the time. Tonight it seemed less funny.

The moment his head reached the pillow, sleep abandoned him.

He lay wide-eyed, staring at the half-visible ceiling. A metal bar had been placed across his forehead and secured at each side with bolts: these, as he remained stubbornly in position on the mattress, tightened themselves remorselessly, crushing his skull. He bore it until he was forced to sit up. The text of his interview with Appleby ticked through his mind: the young milkman's lean pessimistic face and broad-vowelled speech confronted him in the silence, blocking sleep's advance. Softly he swore.

Climbing strenuously out of bed, he drank half a

tumbler of water, performed exercises, sat on a rock-hard wooden stool at the other side of the room, glared at the bedclothes until their allure seemed irresistible. He crawled back, shivering. He tried not to think about his head.

The metal bar had lifted but was hovering, poised to fall back in a grinding of screw threads if he dropped his guard. Think of deep space. Myriads of stars in an inky vortex. Drifting, suspended in the void. Sinking. A tumult of distant voices.

The door beyond the archway at the end of the landing opened to his touch, admitting him to a spiral stairway. He glided upwards. At the top was a passage, barely head-height. Walls and ceiling pressed in upon him like a coal-face.

He groped along. Light came from a remote slit, a narrow vertical oblong some way ahead: the glimmer was sepia, sickly, like the pumping of third-grade oil. Its distance was deceptive. Twice he thought it within reach: both times he stretched an arm to find nothing.

The distant voices chattered, a cage of jungle monkeys.

He considered returning to find the waiter. Then he remembered. He was in this alone. No one could help him now. But instantly the waiter was at his elbow, peering earnestly into his face. 'Good to hear the bustle again, sir,' wheezed the old fellow.

'Stay back,' ordered Larkin tersely. 'You might get hurt.'

The waiter chuckled and hurried on. His bent spine and curved legs bobbed and scuttled between the walls, masking the oblong of bilious light but creating the corona of an eclipse. It was something to make for.

Striding hard, Larkin made his tone severe. 'Leave this to me.'

Something held him back. Ahead and above him the monkeys gibbered; he knew now that the waiter had reached them, that the door was swinging to, that he wouldn't be in time. He struggled forward. The tilt of the floor increased: with every pace he took the gradient sharpened and the darkness intensified. A chill gust swept across him. He started to topple back.

He lay with a hammering heart, the breeze from the open window on his arms. Thrusting them beneath the clothes, he listened.

Echoes of the dream knocked about his brain. The voices had been there, calling confusedly, up to the instant he awoke: now that he was concentrating, starting to perspire, all was stillness; and yet . . .

The breeze remained cold on his face. He thought about closing the window. Turning on his right side, he buried himself. Warmth crowded in. He fell asleep, and dreamed of Bunty.

CHAPTER X

'SHOULDN'T TAKE LONG,' said Smut with an affectionate glance at a bill-poster which stated: 'Phantom Inn— Police Appeal.' He turned into the newsagent's. 'Might be a later edition,' he explained, and vanished.

Larkin waited, shuddering in the blast. He had eaten little breakfast and yet both his head and stomach felt distended, swollen by imprudent living. When Smut emerged with *The Times* he told him, 'I'll come with you to the Press conference, but after that I'm off for the day.'

Smut gave him a close look. 'Up to you, Jim. You know best what's good for you.'

'I wonder.'

'Come to dinner tonight,' Smut said suddenly. 'Carrie's itching to meet you.'

'That'll be nice. You won't mind if I steal off early-ish?'

'You won't get a chance to do otherwise, sonnie. The Goulds have a system. Prior to guests arriving, every clock in the house is shoved forward an hour. At what appears to be eleven o'clock, Mrs Gould rises to her feet, yawns massively, and accidentally drops one of the cheaper wine-glasses on to the coffee table. The ensuing furore shatters the mood along with the glassware, and this promising development is reinforced, prompt on cue, by squawks from our trained brood upstairs; by which time the guests are too demoralized to do other than retreat, casting mystified glances at their watches. Rarely known to fail.'

'I should think not.'

'Except once, when we were entertaining my boss. Having failed to notice our clock striking the witching hour, he deftly caught Carrie's wineglass in mid-air and was so pleased with himself that he stayed on till one a.m. by his own timepiece, reminiscing over past triumphs on the cricket field and finishing off the whisky bottle. We'd no reserve plan to fall back on at the time—but we have now, laddie, we have now.'

'I can't say I haven't been warned.'

'You don't look yourself, Jim. Bad night?'

'A puzzling one.'

Smut lifted his chin. When Larkin didn't enlarge he said forbearingly, 'Mossop's having sleepless nights too.'

They had reached the Stag's front porch. Larkin paused.

'Tell me something. What kind of—'

'What?' said Smut curiously.

Larkin was looking across his shoulder along the main street. A milk van was stationary at the kerb outside a distant shop. 'Never mind,' he said, 'I've had my answer. Let's get inside, hear what Mossop has to say.'

The Stag's interior looked much as it had before. Everything had been kept in its place, including the menu cards on the dining-room tables. Among the journalists roaming the rooms, supervised by constables, Elaine Hurst stood out like barley sugar in a dish of salt biscuits. Flashbulbs exploded at intervals. On the window side of the lounge, Chief Inspector Mossop had been talked into posing with a pair of assistants: the three of them were making futile efforts to appear to be investigating a blank wall. This went on for some time. Retiring to a seat near the immense inglenook, Larkin sucked a peppermint. Gavin Foster, whom he had not seen at breakfast, bade him good morning.

'Fearfully Olde Englishe,' he observed, slapping the ornamental brickwork. 'Do people still go for these places? Me, I've a totally shameless preference for the stainless steel and plastic that we're all supposed to despise.'

Larkin said it was no doubt a question of what one was after.

'Comfort for the body, you mean, or balm for the soul? I know which I'd choose. You can keep your ancient inns of Britain. Though I will say,' Foster conceded grudgingly, 'they've melded the extremes quite nicely in this joint. Some kitchen they've got back there. Seen it? Gadgeteer's delight.'

Larkin said he hadn't gone around examining the Stag's culinary equipment.

'Worth a look. Every bloody electrical aid you can imagine, down to the meat-mincer. Someone with a power complex must have designed it.'

'Perhaps the Sandersons went up in a shower of sparks.'

Foster considered this. 'Put it to the chief inspector,' he advised. 'He's crazy for ideas. Hullo, I think we're off.'

They followed Mossop and his team through to the dining-room to form a semi-circle about the central table. The detective opened with some general remarks. A sergeant handed round prints. It appeared that the police, after initial scepticism as to the validity of the case, were now treating it as a major inquiry and were inviting the media to help. Foster nudged Larkin's ribs.

'The photos you now have of the Sandersons,' said

Mossop, 'are the best available. Taken less than a year ago at a luncheon of the Chamber of Trade. That of Maisie Longton dates back about ten months. According to her aunt it's a good likeness, better than the one that's managed to appear already in some of the national papers . . .' Smut's foot tapped Larkin's calf-muscle. 'We know we can count on their being used as widely as possible.' Mossop gazed around. 'If any of these people are seen anywhere in the country, it goes without saying we should like to be put in touch with them. The reason for their disappearance is far from clear. What we are investigating . . .'

The assembled Pressmen listened politely until there was a chance to throw questions. Mossop fielded them smartly.

'It's true to say,' he told Ian Butler, 'that nothing whatsoever has been found in the inn to suggest any-thing—untoward. All in excellent order.'

'So the *Mary Celeste* tag,' put in Elaine Hurst sweetly, 'is hardly inappropriate.'

Mossop paused. 'There are parallels,' he agreed briefly.

'Except,' Elaine proceeded in sugared accents, 'for the reappearance of one of the four—thanks, I believe, to a colleague of ours.' Several pairs of eyes switched towards Larkin. 'We're told she's suffering from amnesia. Does this still apply?'

'It does,' said Mossop.

'But you're hoping she'll regain her memory and be able to help you?'

'Of course.'

'Can I confirm where she is now?'

'At home,' said Mossop after hesitation. 'We hope the

familiar environment may help her. Her sister's looking after her, and a police officer is with them.'

Gavin Foster said, 'Has thought been given to perhaps bringing her here, in the hope that it might stir—'

'It's being kept in mind.' Mossop glanced at a deputy. 'If her doctor agrees, and we believe it could bear fruit, we'll certainly consider that.'

'Any theories as to what made her do it?'

'You mean,' said Mossop blandly, 'how she came to fall into the stream?'

Foster moved impatiently. 'Off the record, Chief Inspector. Everyone knows she jumped. Is there no clue to what motivated her?'

Mossop thought it over. He said, 'One possibility—'

Ballpoints took up position. He went on, 'Her sister, Mrs Thorpe, tells us that her sister was extremely worried about the state of trade here at the inn, and hence her own position.'

The ballpoints skidded to a halt. Foster said in a discouraged voice, 'I see. Great.'

'Which could mean,' piped Elaine audibly, 'she'd got the push that morning.'

Mossop looked disapproving. 'This can only be surmise, and I must ask you to treat most of what I say as non-attributable background. We've no evidence to suggest that Miss Cotteridge was paid off that morning. If we had, and if this accounted for her—her accident, it doesn't account for the disappearance of the Sandersons or Miss Longton.'

Ian Butler leaned forward.

'Certain rumours are circulating in the town, Chief Inspector. Can we take it that these are being assessed in the light of events, or do we—'

Mossop spoke crisply. 'In an investigation of this nature—any nature—we go by facts. That's all I can say.'

The wind brought scatters of rain, and Larkin reached late afternoon in a state of some disorder.

On leaving Smut after the Press conference he had taken the MG to the end of the road on a hillside where it became a track which puttered to a standstill at the lip of a lake. Here he had browsed on foot for an hour, waiting vainly for the astringent breeze to galvanize his cerebral processes. A sense of unreality besieged him. It was as though he had two thumbs and seven fingers about some reassuring handrail of normality while the eighth finger remained unaccountably idle. Someone or something was needed to guide it to its place—but who or what? He felt disorientated. Striving to perceive the beauty of the lake that he knew must be there, he saw only a scene of bleakness to which the moaning wind was a requiem. When the hour was up he left the car and began to walk.

He lunched at a pub on the far side of the water. The red-haired woman who sold him beef sandwiches confided that the police had been around the lake the day before but had discovered nothing. Which wasn't surprising, was it? Because it was obvious what had happened.

'Tell me,' he invited.

Why, the Sandersons had got deep into debt and done a bunk. 'They're not the first round these parts, *and* they won't be the last. *And* I don't know as I blame them. Trade's that poor.'

'But what about Maisie Longton?'

'That little piece? She's seen her chance, gone off to

one of the big towns. Plenty of excitement and boys. That's all they're after, any of 'em.'

Larkin forbore to ask how the triple vanishing trick had been accomplished in broad daylight. He drank a half-pint of cider, smoked an unsatisfactory pipe, re-read the Press accounts of his own part in denying eternity the premature arrival of Hilda, studied hazily the double-column picture of Maisie that the *Citizen*, fed by Smut, had hung in the centre of a page; and advanced nowhere.

At closing time, armed with directions from the red-haired landlady, he set out for Black Tor Beacon, a celebrated landmark. An hour's struggle along the bed of a runnel took him to a region of driving mist and ultimately to a small pyramid of stones, oozing moss and moisture, that marked the summit. Light-headed, wondering why he had bothered, he leaned against it to suck a peppermint.

His hair became drenched. Through the loosely-stacked boulders of the pyramid the passage of air made whistling and sucking sounds, as though someone were trying to speak. The impression grew on him until he stood away, moved to the rear of the pile, feeling a fool. He even spoke aloud. 'Anyone here?'

A shape seemed to stir in the murk. He went towards it. His foot twisted on a stone and he fell flat. Laughter rang in his ears.

Scrambling up, he peered around. Nothing animate was to be seen. There were just the stones, the wind, the trickling of water. He started to feel dizzy. Some deep breathing helped; after that he pocketed his frozen hands, found the runnel again and set off shakily downhill.

CHAPTER XI

'HONEST TRUTH,' said Caroline. 'No one's ever had a word to say against them. Not till now.'

'Which in a town this size,' added Smut, 'is tantamount to canonization.'

'Not that they'd have claimed to be saints.'

'I don't know. A lot of us imagine we are.' Smut grinned wickedly. 'The rest of us have given up trying.'

'You speak for yourself.'

'What exactly,' asked Larkin, sipping pale coffee, 'are the rumours?'

Caroline, a large tawny woman in her late thirties, as robust as her younger sister was insubstantial, glanced at her husband with a gleam in her dark eyes.

'Which one do I give him?'

'Nothing buckshee,' said Smut with emphasis. 'Cash deal only. This Larkin character, I tell you, gathers all the dross and beats it into gold—so no handouts.'

'I can't be commercial,' declared Caroline, 'when there's a spicy tale to be told. It's sheer pleasure. Let's see. There's the one about Mr Sanderson doing away with Mrs Sanderson in the cellar and running off to the Bahamas with Maisie. I think that holds the track record at the moment.'

'Does it allow,' inquired Smut, 'for the fact that Mrs Sanderson's body hasn't been found in the cellar?'

'Oh, nobody bothers about details like that. Why spoil a good plot?'

Larkin said dreamily, 'It's a challenge to the average imagination. Most of them don't stretch to accommodating practical aspects. A given situation . . .' He lost the thread of what he was saying.

Smut, with a quick glance, took him up. 'People don't want to rationalize, you mean? In case it interferes with their preconceptions. Yeah, well, we've some classic material here. Teenage beauty queen glides between husband and wife in old dark house . . . which is what the Stag is if you stand back and look at it. That's all: finish. The details can be tied in later.'

Caroline frowned. 'I don't think people are as gormless as that. They work it out. I mean, take this rumour I was mentioning. No one specifically thinks he knocked her off in the cellar; that was just my way of putting it. There are various ways it could have been done. He could have—'

'My wife,' said Smut in apology, 'is an inveterate watcher of the box.'

'All there is to do,' she retorted, 'while I wait for you to get home. More coffee, Jim? I still say that what people are discussing is a perfectly reasonable supposition, and as likely as anything else.'

'Where does Hilda fit in?'

'Hilda? She saw something, or suspects something.'

'That drove her to suicide?'

'She was nuts about Sanderson herself,' said Caroline without hesitation. 'Well, why not? Middle-aged spinster and good-looking ex-tank commander with greying temples—brother, there's chemistry for you. When she saw it was Maisie he was after, it turned her head. She was neurotic already. With the final crisis—'

'Is this all part of the myth?'

'I'm just giving it to you as I hear it. That morning, either she witnessed the crime or guessed what had occurred: her brain snapped entirely and off she wandered—'

'To chuck herself in a stream twenty-four hours later. Where was she in the meantime?'

'Roaming wild. You may laugh,' said Caroline severely, 'but I've read sillier things in the Sunday papers, and not necessarily the messy ones.'

'Jim probably wrote some of them. I dunno,' said Smut uproariously. 'Good few gaping holes in the oilcloth. Why beat his wife's brains out? He could have just gone off with the girl. Why leave the car? They'd have taken it, surely. Why were none of them seen?'

'One point that has been raised . . .'

'What's that, Jim?'

'Hilda's choice of a place to jump. Miles of riverbank, and I must have been virtually the sole person about that morning. And yet she presents herself ten yards from me to take a dive.'

Smut thought about it. 'What made you choose that spot for lunch?'

'Pleasant stretch of grass, open from the lane.'

'There you are, then. Suited Hilda too.'

'I hadn't looked at it that way,' Larkin admitted. He turned to Caroline. 'Do you know Hilda's sister?'

'Mrs Thorpe? She and her husband used to live near my parents, they knew them very well. Then they took this cottage outside the town—the Thorpes did, I mean. Then Mr Thorpe was killed in a farming accident.'

'After that,' said Smut,' she had Hilda to live with her.'

'Up to then Hilda had lived on her own?'

'That's right, in the house her parents left. Just back of the Royal. Handy for her work at the Stag.'

'Wouldn't she have been better staying there?'

G

'Probably found the upkeep beyond her. And she may have found it lonely. And I expect Mrs Thorpe was lonely.'

'Rather a solitary person, Hilda?'

Caroline glanced at her husband. 'She's supposed to have had this rather tragic love affair when she was very young. Blighted her life or something.'

'It was the butcher,' said Smut.

'It was not. All he's interested in are his sirloin cuts and his darts. You'd have to ask my mother, she knows more about it than I do and she'd adore to tell you. Anyhow,' said Caroline, wrenching apart a box of petit-fours and handing them round, 'after the shattered romance I guess the Stag was Hilda's refuge. She met people there. Strangers from outside, and there was always the hope . . .'

'Up until the slump,' said Smut.

'The slump,' Larkin repeated. He rubbed his eyes. 'Returning to the Sandersons . . . could I take another look at the photo?'

Smut passed him one of the prints distributed that morning. It showed a couple in evening dress seated at a table, twisting in their chairs to smile up into the magnesium glare. The man's strong face under receding black hair was lined and pitted but relaxed; the expression of his wife was alert and happy. 'Her hair,' Smut remarked, 'looks darker there than it is. She's more a mousy-auburn, if you can imagine.'

Larkin nodded and continued to gaze. Mrs Sanderson's face was oval and pretty beneath a pyramidical hairdo presumably acquired for the occasion: she looked, even in two dimensions, like a small neat person whom it would be hard to fluster. He handed back the print.

'Good-looking pair. Your photo?'

'Do me a favour. This was taken by some Lifton nut who shall be nameless. Mossop found it in their living-room, inside a drawer.'

Caroline peered over his shoulder. 'It'll be in tomorrow's papers?'

'And today's evenings. All Mossop has to do now is sit back and wait for the false sightings in London, Newcastle and Glasgow.'

'What's known about the Sandersons?' Larkin inquired. 'I mean before they came here.'

Smut considered. 'They'd a lot of experience, I believe, in the hotel trade. Ran a place in the Cotswolds. And as I said, he was in the war. Eighth Army. They'd both be round about fifty now.'

'Children?'

'Not to anyone's knowledge.'

'According to Lydia at the post office,' said Caroline, 'Mrs Sanderson told her once that having no children was their one big regret.'

'That's it, then,' pronounced Smut. 'Why look further? The great sorrow. Build-up of resentment. Enter Maisie. Whack, bang, here she is, nubile maiden for him to try again with. Problem: fluffy Mrs S. in the way. Answer: direct action to—'

'Shut up, Smutty. The way you go on.'

'Me? Who initiated the hypothesis? There's a phrase for you, Jim, you can have that for free. Still feeling under the weather?'

With a start, Larkin removed hands from eyes. 'Just a couple of disturbed nights.'

'Move in here, you faggot. We've a spare bed. Carrie can practise some recipes on you.'

'Yes, Jim, do come. The kids'll love to have you around.'

'You're both very kind and I appreciate the offer.' Larkin yawned. 'I think if you don't mind I'll put up with the Royal for another night or two.'

'Doesn't want to lose sight of Irene,' Smut said to his wife.

'Not only that. I'm surrounded by Pressmen there, don't forget. I can keep my ears open on your behalf.'

'The altruism of the man.' Smut regarded him with affectionate cynicism. 'When I think how I had to talk you into taking an interest . . .'

'You did a very good job,' said Larkin.

Irene was still on duty. She looked as haggard as he felt, but she managed a smile.

'Enjoy yourself at Carrie's?'

'An eatable meal at last,' he said gravely.

'I'll tell Mr Potter you said that.'

'Wait till I've paid my bill.' He accepted his room key. 'Toiling late tonight?'

'Mike usually looks after things from about nine, but he said he'd other jobs to do.' She moved off to attend to a man from the *Mirror* who was asking about phone messages.

Behind Larkin a voice said, 'All pouring in at once. Must indicate unanimity of purpose—or something.'

A familiar countenance dimpled at him from inside a crimson mackintosh hood tied girlishly beneath the chin. From deep within long-concealed reserves of resilience and fortitude he answered with an acceptable version of a smile. 'My present purpose,' he informed her, 'is to lay my hands on about ten hours' uninterrupted sleep.'

'You've obviously had a *ruinous* day. Room five, dear, if you wouldn't mind. Not more rescue operations, I trust?'

'Footslogging, chiefly.'

'You? With that marvellous little MG standing idle? Don't come it, Jim. I've just watched you get out of it.'

'Nevertheless, I'm here to walk.'

'So you said before and I didn't believe you then. You want to know what I think? I think you're unearthing all kinds of super seaminess from under the tranquil surface and hugging it to yourself, you naughty man.' Accepting her key with a gracious palm, Elaine turned on him the full power of her dimples. 'You know, Jim, the *Examiner* pays awfully well.'

'In that case,' said Larkin, 'one would think its employees could make their own inquiries and not have to pester other people.'

She blinked, stared at him a moment, then forced a laugh. 'You sound tired, darling. Perhaps you do need that sleep.' She stilted off to the lift.

'That was telling her,' said Irene, returning.

He thrust hair away from his eyes. 'I'm not at my best with round-faced viragos. All the same I should keep my temper. Damn. Good night, Irene.'

'Jim . . .'

'Yes?'

'Still being disturbed by noises at night?'

'A little,' he said after a pause. 'Why?'

Glancing around, she moved closer. 'I spoke to Mike about it,' she said confidentially, 'and his behaviour was rather odd.'

'In what way?'

'Well . . . I pointed out that it was only the attic rooms above you, which we never use. So he turned a bit snappy. Why bother him in that case, he said, it was just your fancy. I said I didn't think you were the fanciful type—'

'Thanks for that. Though I'm increasingly less sure of its accuracy.'

She looked troubled. 'You don't look it to me. And Smut says . . . Anyhow, this afternoon while things were quiet I went up there to have a peep. At least I tried to go up there.'

Larkin looked at her. 'But?'

'The door to the attic stairs was locked. It's not normally. I went back downstairs and asked Vic—our old waiter, you know—if he'd a key, and he said he thought Mike had the only one. But I'm sure that's not right.'

Larkin thought for a moment.

'Who,' he asked, 'mainly runs the hotel? Mr Philip Potter, or Mike?'

'Mr Potter sees to the catering—that's his speciality. And he'd have the last word on any major decision, I suppose. But Mike's really the manager.'

'Ambitious?'

'Who, Mike?' She pursed her lips. 'He wants to make a go of the Royal, get it back on its feet. He's told me that himself.'

'The fishing slump must have been a bad blow to him.'

Irene hesitated. 'Give him his due, Mike's a fighter. He'll dream up ways to pull back the customers, of that I'm sure.'

'No doubt he will,' said Larkin dryly. 'The Royal's a good place for dreaming.' He smiled at her. 'Good night again, and thanks.'

He took the lift to the second floor. A symptom this,

he reflected uneasily, of moral as well as physical decline. But the procedure had the merit of averting possible confrontations on the stairs. He emerged from the lift to be met by the rewarding sight of Ian Butler, swathed in a vivid gold gigantic house-robe, tiptoeing from the bathroom to his bedroom door with an immense key dangling from his right forefinger and a copy of *Penthouse* beneath his left armpit. Larkin said cheerily, 'Night, old boy.' Butler tossed him a scowl and a gesture, let himself in with a rattle, closed the door, rattled again. Silence followed.

Larkin was alone on the landing. Treading gently, he continued past his own door and three others to the curtained archway, and stepped through. He glanced back.

With a quick movement he released the cord holding one of the curtains. The material swung down. Concealed by it, he approached the door facing the archway and tested the handle.

As Irene had said, it was locked. Taking out his pocket knife he inserted it cautiously, worked it about.

The spring was stiff or rusty. He dropped to his knees, bringing his eyes down to the level. The light was poor. The exploration of the blade seemed to achieve nothing beyond a series of futile prods. Then abruptly the point of it slid between opposing metal surfaces, found a purchase. He levered.

Suddenly the light improved. He was puzzled, because the door had not yet opened. The significance dawned on him belatedly and he turned his head. Michael was looking down at him from the archway.

The younger man said politely, 'I'm afraid you won't find a bathroom through there.'

Larkin palmed the knife. 'I was afraid I'd lost my

bearings.' He straightened up. 'I'm looking for the shower.'

Standing aside, Michael pointed back.

'There, where it says "Shower".' He smiled, but his eyes were cold. 'We'll have to get those letters repainted, a little larger.'

'My fault entirely.' Larkin came away from the door. 'I'm sleepy, not focusing too well. I came right past it.'

'Easy to do.' Elaborately Michael made way for him. When Larkin was clear of the curtain he re-hooked the cord with an adroit movement; then with an apparent change of mind he released both cords so that the curtains fell to meet in the centre, blocking the archway. 'Just to prevent further mistakes,' he said. 'We've lost enough people in this town already.'

'Three too many,' Larkin agreed. 'Good night to you.'

He marched into the shower room.

No towels were provided. After five minutes he came out, unmoistened: Michael had gone. The curtains were now laced together, top, bottom and centre. Returning to his room, Larkin undressed and fell into bed. He lay sleepless for an hour, listening to the thumps.

CHAPTER XII

ONE OF the numerous stories in the nationals next morning captured his attention.

Signalled by a front-page panel, it appeared on the centre spread of the *Citizen* under Ian Butler's byline: it was headed *Is This Why Three People Vanished Into The Blue?*

He read it over a late breakfast. The mass of the Fleet Street invading forces had doused their hangovers in black coffee and left for the day's round-up; he had the dining-room almost to himself. At a window table sat a solitary reporter from the *Telegraph* completing the *Guardian* crossword. It showed, thought Larkin, an open mind.

Ian Butler had plunged straight in.

> Police probing the 'Phantom Inn' affair are considering a theory that the root of it lies not in crime, but in *Publicity*.
>
> They are not saying much. Officially, that is. But privately they do not dispute that this baffling occurrence in the West Country uplands *could* be less sinister—and more tiresome—than was at first assumed.
>
> Look at the *background* . . .'

This, Butler had sketched in with some skill before proceeding:

> Now take a look at a few facts that have come my way.
>
> Fact: The Stag Inn had been doing badly. Patronage had slumped.

Fact: The drop-off dates from two years back.

Fact: Two years ago the stock of fish in local streams succumbed (allegedly) to pollution. For whatever reason, the fish have not returned.

Fact: The bulk of the Stag's guest list were anglers.

Shuffle this hand and what are we left with?

Buttering a finger of toast, Larkin bit off a half. He read on carefully.

The inescapable conclusion is that the Stag's owners faced trouble. Big trouble.

The catastrophic drop in takings was likely to last as long as the fish famine persists—and experts here tell me that no one can say for sure how long that might be.

Industry is growing in the area. This means effluent. Strict controls? Undoubtedly—but some will always slip the net. Outlook: murky.

So, for the Stag, what was needed was an alternative attraction. In some way it had to get known, to hit the headlines.

Hence, police think, the vanishing trick. Always riveting. Never a flop.

And not just another 'missing persons' story, but a latter-day *Mary Celeste* for good measure.

Opinion, too, is gaining ground that the incident involving 57-year-old Hilda Cotteridge, a fourth member of the staff, may not be directly related.

She was, I understand, already of a morbid or even neurotic disposition. Her fall into a nearby stream could have been—shall we say?—coincidental.

All this will inspire an official denial. But one thing is for sure.

If and when the Sandersons and Maisie Longton

do show up, Chief Inspector Mossop and his hard-working team will have some searching questions for them.

Oh, and one other thing. The publicity is already fantastic.

Larkin re-read the article. After that he scanned the contributions of Butler's rivals. He poured himself a third cup of weak tea, fought the urge to add sugar, succumbed, drank the feeble mixture to the midway level, took a codeine tablet for his headache, sat back in his chair and stared out at the sun-lightened street.

He arrived back in town at four-thirty. Parking the MG outside the Stag, he walked across to the porch and rang. Eventually a constable answered.

No, the chief inspector wasn't there.

'Do you know where I can find him?'

'Back at HQ, like as not. Other end of Main Street, bear left, carry on for half a mile. Would you be a Press reporter?'

'Not if I could help it,' said Larkin. Returning to the car, he drove off.

The alacrity with which Mossop made himself available was a surprise. Having given his name, Larkin was conducted instantly to a suffocatingly warm room at the rear of the police station, a pair of slated cottages knocked into one. Passing the main office, he observed three or four shirt-sleeved men seated at telephones on a central table. One was talking mono-syllabically into a mouthpiece.

At Larkin's entry Mossop rose, but said nothing. They stood surveying one another. Tiring of this, Larkin said tentatively, 'Probably you don't remember me: I'm James Larkin, who first notified—'

'What makes you think I'd forget, Mr Larkin? I've been expecting you.'

'You have?'

Larkin scratched his neck. Turning, Mossop walked to the rear of his chair, placed both hands on the back of it and lifted himself several inches. Returning to the floor, he eyed Larkin in a speculative manner.

'Can't offer you anywhere to sit, I'm afraid. Had this room rigged up for me at short notice. Frightful inconvenience we've all been put to, one way and another.'

'I can imagine.'

Backing to a window, Larkin supported himself by its ledge. The ache in his legs had ascended to his lower spine; a sensation of light-headedness was becoming a problem.

'You can, eh?' Mossop hummed to himself, performed a second vertical press-up, landed again.

Larkin's patience began to ebb. He said, 'I came to see you—'

'Aha.' Mossop stopped humming, returned to his chair and looked businesslike. 'I was about to consult you on that. Want to make another statement?'

'If you like. Or perhaps it needn't be so official as that. I only want to give some information—'

'I'm all in favour of it.'

'What really brings me here,' said Larkin, counting to eight, 'is the article that appeared in today's *Citizen*. I don't know if you've seen it?'

Mossop nodded impassively.

'Nor can I guess your reaction . . .'

Mossop didn't enlighten him.

'However, you'll have followed the line of reasoning. Now, from the few inquiries I've made myself, I conclude that Butler's surmises aren't necessarily— necessarily—'

Larkin put a hand to his eyes. The chief inspector had commenced to sway in front of him, which would have been less alarming if the desk hadn't joined in. When he looked again, Mossop was surveying him with a curiously intent expression. The swaying had ceased. Sagging further on to the ledge, Larkin tried to recapitulate.

'What the article was suggesting . . .'

No use. Blankly he returned the other's stare, hunting through his mind for what it was in particular that had motivated this visit. Flashes reached him of the day he had spent, like shutter-glimpses thrown upon a sheet. He recalled walking. Eating little. Fixing a course of action: what course? Nothing that now showed itself seemed to dovetail with anything else. Mossop was again on his feet.

'Perhaps I can help you, Mr Larkin. You came here to tell us that Ian Butler's theories are in fact—er— facts?'

That was it. He nodded, shutting his eyes.

'And what makes you so certain?'

Since it was less taxing that way, he kept his eyelids down. 'Number of things . . . vital factors . . .'

A seeping of patience from Mossop's tone was detectable.

'Why don't we stop beating about the bush? You've come here, Mr Larkin, to tell us about your part in this? Eh?'

He did his best to follow that. And to remain upright. The room temperature was intolerable.

'What do you say?' The voice was loud in his ears.

He clutched at the ledge. 'May I sit down?'

A scraping noise. With blinding distinctness he saw Mossop dragging his chair. He was helped into a seating posture. His knees were pushed apart, his head was thrust down between them. He felt sick.

'. . . simply the initial alert? Press furore . . . What about the actual spiriting away?'

The queries made remarkably little sense. He found he was weakly shaking his head. 'You'll have to let me rest . . .'

'Sit quietly for a while.'

The brandy had a rapid effect. A window had been opened; gratefully he breathed in and out. He sat erect.

'Do apologize . . . Never done that before. Must have walked a little too far today.'

'Thinking things over, possibly?'

'Well—yes. I wasn't sure what I was justified in telling you. Had to sort things out.'

A movement made him turn his head. Behind him a police officer in shirt-sleeves was noting something on a pad.

'More brandy, Mr Larkin?'

'Thank you, no. Fine now.'

'You've been under strain.'

'So they kept telling me. That's why I came away.'

'Why you came away,' repeated Mossop. He had occupied Larkin's former position at the window. 'It was all arranged, then?'

'Oh yes. As I told you, I was booked in at the Stag. Which is why it was so—'

'Let's take it at walking pace. You make your living, don't you, by uncovering bizarre stories?'

'You could say that. But what—'

'A fair living?'

'Variable. I still don't see—'

'Let me just put the questions, Mr Larkin. You came in to help us, after all; you said so yourself. The build-up intrigues me. Did your partner make the Stag booking or did you?'

'I did, at his suggestion. He thought—'

'He thought you might both stand to gain a lot? He runs the business side of the agency, I understand.'

'Yes, but—'

'So you and he and the Sandersons,' said Mossop thoughtfully, 'were in touch well before this occurrence. Right. Would you like now to tell me about it?'

'If you'll allow me to insert a word,' Larkin said angrily. 'Frankly, the relevance of all this escapes me. Can't we take it from the time of my arrival?'

'Let's do that.' Mossop made himself comfortable. A rustle of notepaper came from behind.

'All this preliminary chat . . . it's gone out of my head. I've not been sleeping well—'

'I can understand that. You've had a lot on your mind,' said the chief inspector with unction. 'Why don't we go back to question and answer? Easier, more satisfactory all round. All right now? First question. How did you get them away from the inn?'

CHAPTER XIII

LARKIN'S IMMEDIATE REACTION was to laugh. The fury that was his secondary response caused the sound to emerge as a yelp. Mossop looked at him in surprise.

'It's a simple question.'

'Simple?' Larkin choked. 'It's half-witted. I'm speechless. I don't know what to say.'

'Say the truth,' Mossop recommended.

Realization was flooding Larkin with a sense of bemusement. He felt breathless. The formulation of words, the acquisition of wind to utter them, were tasks momentarily beyond him. Mossop leaned forward.

'You've told us a little,' he pointed out moderately. 'You may as well do a proper job, describe the detail. Save us all a mint of bother in the long run.'

'You—you imagine I'd something to do with it?'

Acute disappointment submerged Mossop's face.

'Now let's not have instant retractions, Mr Larkin,' he said wearily. 'You've as good as admitted you played a part. What I want to know—'

'How in God's name did you fasten on to an idea like this?'

The other's eyes strayed past him to rest sadly on the officer to his rear.

'You'll be saying next you want to get in touch with your lawyer.'

'I don't possess a lawyer. Why should I need a lawyer?' Larkin was nearly incoherent. 'What am I being accused of? Burying the Sandersons in the back yard and feeding Maisie into the meat slicer?'

Mossop shook a regretful head.

'No need to confuse the issue. We both know what I'm talking about.'

'I don't know what you're talking about, but I'm starting to guess. I—' Larkin's head swam. He paused for some quick, decisive breaths. 'But for feeling below par, I could have avoided all this. You're actually suggesting . . . Wait a bit, let me work it out. I'm supposed to have driven along to the Stag four days ago, spirited the three of them away, installed them in a hideout somewhere, then come back to mastermind the uproar?'

'You're saying it, Mr Larkin.'

'The idea being to give the Stag some marvellous free publicity, and myself the story of the year?'

'You have to admit,' said Mossop with a thin smile, 'the scheme was a triumph on both counts.'

'There was no scheme. Will you believe that? I came to Miltham for a rest—to get away from work, not land myself in more of it. If you want confirmation of that, contact my partner. I can give you the number—'

'I have Mr Feldham's number,' said Mossop calmly. 'We'll be talking to him, never fear. First, though, I want to hear from you. Get away from work, you say. Is this why you've been going around interviewing people?'

Larkin hesitated.

'I did get interested,' he conceded. 'I'm cursed with that sort of nature . . . any mystery represents a challenge. It's my trade. Naturally I got interested. Also very tired and out of sorts. Today especially. Which is why I made up my mind to pass to you anything I've got and wash my hands of it. As I was about to do before you took the wind out of my sails.'

'You still have the opportunity,' Mossop informed him.

'All right. So long as you accept that I'd nothing to do with the basic event.'

'I'm keeping an open mind. I have to look at facts. One indisputable fact is that no one had noticed anything amiss at the Stag until you happened along and reported it.'

'Wouldn't you have reported it?'

'Which was quite some while,' pursued Mossop, 'after your first arrival. Plenty of time to pack the Sandersons and Maisie into your car—'

'A two-seater?'

'—drive them out somewhere and return to set the ball rolling. According to our inquiries, you've gone off by yourself every day since, in the car, with a bundle of newspapers. Keeping them supplied, Mr Larkin? Showing them how the story's going?'

Larkin said with deliberate patience, 'I've been driving out, leaving the car and walking. Exercise, you know. A holiday.'

'Then we have the affair of Hilda Cotteridge—'

'We do indeed. Am I supposed to have organized that as well?'

'For a man peacefully intent on a week's sabbatical,' remarked Mossop, examining the ceiling, 'you seem to have blundered into both incidents in an extraordinarily unlucky way. Or doesn't ill-fortune come into it?'

For a few moments Larkin was silent.

'I can't account for the Hilda business. She must have just happened to choose that spot—'

'Of course she did: because it was pre-selected, wasn't it? You and she were in collusion, just as you were with the Sandersons. The whole thing's a set-up, isn't it? A cheap publicity gimmick. Thousands of police man-hours up the spout,' said the chief inspector with bitterness. 'Townsfolk harassed, anxiety created—all for some madcap project to draw the spotlight and fetch in the tourists. New trade for the Sandersons, an exclusive for the Larkfeld Press Agency. A neat double. How long was it planned to last?'

Larkin had his temper under wraps. He surveyed Mossop with resolute indulgence.

'May I say, Chief Inspector, I think you're right about the set-up?'

'Thank you so much.'

'And wrong about the machinery. Nothing to do with me, nor my partner. And I think we can leave Hilda out of it, too.'

'Oh, you do? Very good then. We'll do that, certainly.' Sarcasm pulsed in the other's larynx. 'Provided, of course, you can give us one or two trifling reasons why we should take your word for it?'

'The best reason,' Larkin observed, 'would be the discovery of the missing trio, I take it?'

Mossop regarded him almost benignly from the window ledge. 'Second thoughts, Mr Larkin?'

'Not in the way you mean.' He was maintaining control with mounting difficulty. 'I'm debating whether to offer you the information I was proposing to give, that's all.'

'Withholding of essential information,' said Mossop slowly, 'is an offence.'

'You don't need to tell me. I've some experience of the law.'

'So I understand.' Mossop looked again at his deputy, who from the sound of it was covering sheets of note-paper at an impressive rate.

Larkin gave him a sharp glance. 'Is that intended to imply something?'

Detaching himself from the window, Mossop strolled to his desk and picked up a typed slip.

' "James Larkin," ' he read. ' "Nineteen sixty-four: two years for manslaughter. Released July nineteen sixty-five, after maximum remission." ' He gazed across. 'Or have we mistaken the identity?' he inquired politely.

Larkin gazed back.

'No. You're absolutely right.'

Mossop seemed to have expected more. Laying down the slip, he stood looking at it.

'You still insist I should place great weight on what you say?'

Larkin stood.

'I insist on nothing. Except my right to say nothing if I choose. Am I free to go?'

The junior officer rose hurriedly, but Larkin was past him, at the door. Mossop moved to the front of the desk.

'You said you'd some things to tell us.'

Larkin turned. 'But you wouldn't put much weight on them, would you, Chief Inspector? So why go to the bother?' Opening the door, he walked out.

CHAPTER XIV

Driving back, he noticed that the windscreen was misting. All steamed up, he thought. Try a neutralizing approach. Look at the funny side. By the time he reached the Royal he had overpowered the resentment, crushed it to a smouldering core; but had failed to achieve an inner smile.

Throwing a quick outer one to Irene, he strode to the telephone in the foyer and called Islington.

'Alan? Have the police been on to you yet?'

'What about? Tax arrears?'

'Obviously they haven't. I wondered, because—'

'Why would I have heard from the fuzz?'

Larkin told him.

A profound silence ensued at the distant end. He said mildly, 'Still there, Alan? I thought you'd hung up. What do you think about it?'

'I've progressed beyond thought. I'm just asking myself, in a mechanical sort of way, how a chap like you does it.'

'Does what?'

'I mean, take the life I lead.' Feldham's voice gave an impression of settling itself for an extended discourse. 'Daytime in the office, evenings at home. The odd trip to flick or boozer. Excitement? Novelty? Never on your jack-knife. Now take someone like yourself. Regularly, without visible effort—'

'You're paying for this call.'

'*We're* paying,' his partner amended. 'It's out of the profits, if any, and at this rate there won't be. Forget I

117

said that. You're relaxing, God dammit. Disregard the whole thing. Move to another town. Take an extra week. I was right the first time, you should never have got involved . . .'

'I am involved.'

'Uninvolve yourself, then, and fast. I'll get on to this Mossop myself—'

'Don't do that.'

'—and tell him he's talking through the heels of his regulation-issue size elevens. I'll do better,' Feldham asserted with soaring ferocity, 'I'll issue a comprehensive statement to the nationals—'

'No!' said Larkin, appalled. 'Promise me you won't do that, Alan.'

'I get you. I'm simply to stand by, chewing my knuckles—'

'Should the police get in touch with you, give them soft answers. No point in antagonizing the entire force. My quarrel's with Mossop. For the time being I'm not leaving here . . .'

'Maybe you can't?' asked Feldham significantly.

Larkin said he wasn't certain. 'I don't know how far he intends to take this. I may find it hard to be entirely alone from now on.'

'You say you went along with information. Did you let him have it?'

'No.'

'You going to?'

'Not yet. I'm damned if I see why I should,' said Larkin, dropping his voice as people came downstairs. 'If I do, and it's wrong, he'll think I'm trying to throw dust in his eyes. I shall play it by ear.'

'His or yours?' Feldham snorted for a while. 'I suppose,' he lamented at last, 'I'll have to leave it to your judgment, as usual, and hope it's not been dulled by the soft West Country living. How does a coastal cargo ship appeal to you? Not expensive, lashings of good food, a three-day excursion into the Arctic Circle—'

'Book a voyage yourself,' said Larkin. 'With all this foaming you do, you belong to the high seas. Bye for now.'

He ascended to his room. After lying flat on the bed for half an hour, he had a warm bath. The inner smile broke surface: he remembered what Feldham had said.

He dressed with special care. Did some deep breathing by the open window. Combed his hair. Checked all zips and buttons. When he felt in command of himself and had devoured two peppermints, he went downstairs.

Ian Butler was the hub of attention in the bar. At Larkin's appearance the focus shifted. Taking no notice, he found a space by the sausage container and asked Michael for cider.

'One pint of best Taunton,' said the younger Potter briskly, 'coming up.'

Conversation, which had faltered, lurched back into a stride. Larkin ate a handful of salted biscuits from a dish.

Butler turned to him, 'Evening, Jim. Been sleuthing?'
'Have you?'
'Not to the detriment of my calf-muscles. Saw no reason to slog around today.'

Larkin took a second handful of biscuits. 'I read your very erudite piece this morning. First-rate. Just the conclusion I'd been reaching myself.'

People nearby were listening stealthily. On the corner bench, Elaine Hurst talked with animation to

the young reporter from the *Sun*, whom she appeared
to be giving her undivided attention.

'Great minds, eh, Jim?'

'That must be it.'

Butler paused warily. Then darted. 'I heard the fuzz
were quizzing someone.'

Larkin swallowed the last of the biscuits.

'Me, as a matter of fact.'

'Go on?' Butler made no attempt to sound amazed.
'What did they want out of you?'

'A signed confession, I think.' Larkin's voice reached
every corner. Nobody now was making any pretence
of not listening.

'A confession, for Christ's sake? What of?'

'Mossop seems to think I engineered the entire Stag
affair as a publicity stunt.' Larkin turned his head to
smile across the bar counter at Michael, who was
watching him with a slightly open mouth.

'He must be crackers,' said Butler unconvincingly.

Gavin Foster stepped forward. 'Why pick on you,
Jim?'

'Sensation-hungry features man,' he explained.

'What a load of tripe.'

'You laughed at him, I hope?'

'It's hard to laugh,' said Larkin, 'when your record's
being thrown at you.'

'Record,' Butler repeated cautiously.

'I served two years,' Larkin enunciated clearly, 'for
manslaughter.'

Butler recovered well. 'That's hardly . . . germane to
the issue, I'd have thought. I mean there's no suggestion—'

'I trust not.' Sipping cider, Larkin smiled around. 'If

there were to be, I should naturally sue at once for heavy damages.'

Foster cut into an uneasy silence.

'Come down off it, Jim. The fuzz can't have been serious. They're scratching around.'

'Yes. They left their claw-marks on me.'

'Sign of desperation. They'd read my piece,' said Butler modestly, 'and it gave them ideas. So they tried you first.'

'Why?'

Foster stepped nearer. 'You were first on the spot each time. Admit that, old boy. You turned up at the Stag to find them gone, you rescued the Cotteridge dame—'

'Yes, they gave me all that. I don't see it as a basis for accusations.'

'They're up the creek,' said the *Telegraph* man.

'Possibly,' said Larkin. 'But perhaps less far than we think.'

'Come again?'

'They may have started with me, intending to move on, eliminating as they go.'

'On the stunt theory, you mean?' Butler demanded.

'Certainly. I think it's a sound one. I believe they do.'

'Any orders, gentlemen?' requested Michael.

Smut eyed him keenly but asked no questions. At Larkin's prompting he drove past the unlighted Stag and out of town almost to the road's limit, where he parked on a gravelled inlet. Using the last of his tobacco, Larkin packed and lit a pipe.

He said between puffs, 'I want you to tip off Mossop. If you will.'

'Sure. What do I tell him?'

'What I've told you. After that it's up to him, and if I'm wrong . . .' He jerked the pipe.

'If you're wrong,' mused Smut, 'I'm the silly bugger who has to distribute double rations of scotch and fags at the nick next Christmas.'

'I'll reimburse you. Are you on?'

'You know me, Jim, always fall over myself to oblige. Though I did think you'd want to tell Mossop yourself.'

There was a query in his voice.

'I would have,' said Larkin after a pause, 'if circumstances hadn't altered this afternoon. You may have heard.'

'I've had some garbled account—'

Larkin recounted his experience. 'My standing,' he concluded, 'is appreciably lowered as a result. It seems to me that if I now go back and tell him what I think I know, he'll treat it as an attempt to get myself out of a pickle by spilling half the beans . . . if I make myself clear. Coming from you—'

'Staunch old reliable Gould, the man above suspicion: I see what you mean. I'll tell him, of course, and see how he reacts.' Smut looked at Larkin in the semi-darkness. 'Jim, how did you avoid apoplexy?'

'With difficulty,' he admitted. 'But I suppose there are two sides to it.'

'I'm trying hard to spot the other one. Look, why don't we drive back now—'

'You drive back. I'll walk. The less we're seen together beforehand, the better. You know what to say?'

'Tell me if there's something I've forgotten.' Smut ran through the items. 'A point that bothers me is the correspondence between the Potters and Sandersons and the plastics factory. How did I get to know of it? You made the inquiries there.'

'Fair enough. I told you that bit. Lay stress,' Larkin urged him, 'on the tone of the letters—about the desperate state of trade and so forth. You can say you didn't connect it up until you read Ian Butler's think-piece this morning.'

'Right. And when is Mossop to pounce?'

'Up to him,' said Larkin, 'but what's the point of delay?'

CHAPTER XV

WALKING BACK, he noticed the Stag was in darkness.

On previous nights there had been signs of occupation by Mossop's men. The likelihood was, thought Larkin, that the manpower shortage had now caught up with him. Or was supervision of the place no longer deemed necessary? Studying it from the opposite footway, he heard a sound.

The faintest of scuffs, it seemed to come from the inn's side access.

It was the minimality of the noise that drew him. That, and the years of conditioning. Numbed by fatigue as he was, bruised in spirit by his brush with the law, he rose to a nudge like a puppy to a crust. God help me, he thought gloomily, I'm beyond aid.

Silently he returned to the corner of the inn. He listened; then risked a glance.

Out of range of the nearest street lamp, the drive-in was a well of blackness. Not enticing. He was turning away when he caught the sound again.

He tried some mental sketch-mapping. At the inner end of the drive-in, one turned left beneath an elevated barn into the courtyard: directly ahead stood the annexe. To reach it, one crossed the cobblestones. Some had lifted. He recalled the sound his own feet had made, four days previously. He hesitated; then, slowly and with circumspection, he began to walk.

At the rim of the courtyard he found the darkness not quite absolute: mitigated by the dim reflected glow from the upper windows of buildings beyond the stabling. And by something else. A white beam that dodged and darted across the inn's stonework in the region of the kitchen door.

He remained where he was. The shaft of light travelled, quivered, moved again, came to rest. A hand entered its orbit, seemed to pluck at the wall. Abruptly the light dropped, splashing the cobbles. At walking pace it began to ripple across them towards him.

Noiselessly he changed position.

The light slid past, five feet away. Now he could make out the form behind it. He let it reach the drive-in. Taking three steps forward, he made a grab.

His first step had brushed a cobblestone. The figure reacted instantly, turning to meet the onrush. Larkin heard a gasp, felt the resistance. He tried for an armlock, but the figure squirmed like a reptile, breaking free. Larkin grabbed again. He caught a forearm which was wrenched away, and amid the clatter of receding footfalls a falling object in the gloom snatched at his attention.

In two minds, he teetered and lost his chance. Reaching the mouth of the drive-in, the fleeing figure swung left and vanished. Larkin followed to the footway; the retreating shape was sweeping left again into an alley. He made his decision. Returning to the drive-in, he searched the cobbles by the miserly radiance from the street until he found the thing that had been dropped.

Irene met him in the Royal's foyer.

'Jim, Mrs Thorpe's just phoned. She wanted to speak to you.'

'To me?'

'It's about her sister.' Irene looked dishevelled, as

though she had dealt with too much work, too many queries. 'I couldn't quite make out . . . She wants you to go along.'

'Go along?' He was starting to repeat everything, like a demented parrot. He took a grip on himself. 'To her cottage, does she mean?'

'So I understood.'

Larkin sighed. 'I'll drive over in the morning. Maybe Hilda has found her memory.'

'Mrs Thorpe said, could you go tonight?'

He looked at her blankly. 'It can't be as urgent as that.'

'She sounded upset.' Irene smoothed her hair, drew him aside as two Pressmen strode past. 'She said something about the police and questions they were asking—but some of it I didn't catch.'

He glanced past her at the reception desk. The senior Potter was behind it, talking into the telephone. From the bar drifted a muted clamour. He said, 'Are you free yourself?'

'I was just off home.'

'Would you come with me? I'd be grateful.'

After hesitation she nodded. 'All right. I'll have to phone home first and tell my parents.'

To keep himself awake as they drove out of town on the Launceston road, Larkin sounded her on her home life and ambitions. Her parents lived quietly, she told him, and she would have liked to become a social worker.

'What prevented you?'

'I'd have to have gone away, worked in a bigger town. Then someone else would have had to keep an eye on them. Didn't seem to make sense.'

'Do they need looking after?'

'They're not infirm, exactly,' she said after a pause.

'But they need you?'

'Well . . . I think they like to have me around.'

'They might,' he suggested mildly, 'be pleased to see you become a successful social worker.'

'The Royal's a good substitute,' she said after a further interval. 'Gives me a chance sometimes to indulge my sociological tendencies.'

'You mean help people?'

She laughed. 'Just like a journalist. Subbed down to the core. Smut's always on about that. When you've an inch to fill, he says, why manufacture a yard? Yes, I like helping people.'

'So you'd hate anything to happen to the Royal?'

'Like having to shut? I don't think it would ever happen. Mike's too sharp.'

'You admire him?'

She hesitated. 'I respect his push. I don't particularly care for him as a person.'

Larkin relaxed slightly. He was off guard when she said, 'Smut tells me you had a bad time this afternoon.'

His fingers tightened on the wheel. 'Nothing much. I was merely accused of fabricating the Stag affair.'

She said calmly, 'And did you?'

'You know, it's terrifyingly easy to reach a state of mind where one begins to have doubts. Mossop made it sound quite plausible. In fact I almost wondered why I hadn't.'

'Marvellous idea,' she said unexpectedly. 'Are you still suspect?'

'No doubt.'

'I heard that female viper, the Hurst woman, talking to one of the others earlier this evening.'

'What had dear Elaine to say?'

'She sounded a bit sloshed. From what I could hear, she was crowing over something she'd told Chief Inspector Mossop during the morning.'

'Was she?'

'Your name came up.'

'Did it?'

'You insulted her, didn't you, the night before?'

'I think,' he said presently, 'I may have a quiet word or two with my least favourite lady columnist before I leave.'

He dipped his headlamps in deference to a passing car.

'You don't seem to have had much of a holiday,' observed Irene. 'More like some kind of endurance test.' She took a breath. 'Was Mr Mossop right about your . . . conviction?'

He restored main beam.

'I've answered all your personal questions,' she pointed out.

'True. Well, I was put away for hitting my first wife's boyfriend. He fell and hit his head on the corner of a bookcase.'

'What rotten luck.'

'Possibly—it's hard to say.' He peered through the screen. 'Nearly there, aren't we?'

His headlamps had picked up a police van and a patrol car parked at the foot of a sloping bank at the roadside. Finding space behind them, he helped Irene out. 'Seems they're here in strength.'

The cottage stood alone on the summit of the bank, reached by steep steps between retaining walls. A Ford Escort estate car stood on a gravelled patch connected with the road by a precipitous driveway. Irene pointed to it.

'Mrs Thorpe's.'

Larkin's knock was answered by the tall lean figure of Sergeant Willis, who at sight of them looked nonplussed.

'We're here to see Mrs Thorpe,' Larkin told him pleasantly.

The sergeant peered round. 'Bit awkward at the minute, Mr Larkin . . .'

The face of Mrs Thorpe appeared at his shoulder. She seemed to have been weeping. 'Is it Mr Larkin? I'd like him to come in, please.'

'Now you go back inside, Mrs Thorpe.'

'Are you ordering me about in my own house?'

'I'm only doing what the Chief—'

'Let him in, if you please.'

Willis scowled with indecision. The voice of his superior snapped from within. 'Who is it, Sergeant?'

'Mr Larkin, sir.'

'What the blazes—!'

Mossop arrived from an inner room. He gave Larkin a brief, stupefied appraisal. 'What are you doing here?'

'Waiting on the doorstep,' said Larkin politely, 'to see Mrs Thorpe.'

The chief inspector's mouth worked. He took a pace back.

'Since you're here,' he said curtly, 'you might as well join us.' As Larkin with a courteous nod stepped past, steering Irene by the waist, Mossop turned to Willis. 'Why wasn't he stopped?'

'Miller's just rung through to say . . .' Willis dropped his voice; they muttered together.

Shepherded in a distressed fashion by Mrs Thorpe, Larkin and Irene went through to the inner room. It was large, rectangular, chintzy, and blisteringly hot.

I

The heat came from solid fuel inside an enamelled stove set in the hearth, before which Hilda sat crouched in a tall-backed upholstered chair of excruciating design. Wrapped in a pale blue housecoat, she was gazing into the glow.

Their arrival prompted no change in her posture. She looked huddled, unnaturally still. Watching her from his chair in an alcove beyond the chimney-breast was a scraggy little man of elderly demeanour who glanced up as they entered. Irene nodded to him.

'Hullo, Doctor Parkes.'

Sternly he nodded back. Advancing to the stove, Mrs Thorpe placed a hand on her sister's heavy rounded shoulder and turned to Larkin.

'They've been asking her questions. Virtually *accusing* her.' Her eyes were tearfully bright. 'They say you've admitted everything, Mr Larkin, and so she might as well—'

'All right, Mrs Thorpe.' Mossop had re-entered the room. 'I wasn't aware you'd contacted Mr Larkin . . . was that when you went outside to make tea? Very naughty of you. Never mind. Perhaps it's a good thing he's here. It should enable us—'

'Don't you listen, Mr Larkin,' she said earnestly. 'They're only trying to set a trap.'

'Now that's not fair, Mrs Thorpe.'

'What would you call it, then? Trying to make Hilda say she agreed it all with the Sandersons and Mr Larkin here, and they faked the rescue, and—'

'*Please*, Mrs Thorpe.'

She subsided, sniffing a little. Mossop, the picture of irritated frustration, strode into the centre of the group and glared around. 'As though my job wasn't difficult enough, you people seem determined to trundle obstacles in my path. Mr Larkin: why did you come here?'

'In response to a request from Mrs Thorpe. Why did you?'

Mossop flinched and flushed. 'I've inquiries to make,' he said shortly.

'Of Mrs Thorpe?'

'Of her and her sister. We've yet to—'

'He's been terribly harsh.' Mrs Thorpe squeezed past him to address herself to Irene. 'You know Hilda, dear. She wouldn't do anything dishonest. And yet this—this officer's saying she just *pretended* to be drowning the other day. He says Mr Larkin pulled her out by arrangement. What it's all about I don't begin to understand,' she informed the doctor over her right shoulder, 'but I do know Hilda's in no state to answer his wretched questions. She's still in shock. You can see that's so, can't you, Doctor?'

Doctor Parkes contrived to look both officious and hunted.

'Medically speaking,' he said pompously, 'I feel that Miss Cotteridge is capable of replying to questions *provided* she understands them and doesn't feel threatened by them in any way, and *provided*—'

Mossop turned on him. 'That makes a nonsense of the whole thing.'

'I'm stating my professional view on a matter of—'

'This is why I had you along, Doctor. I've no wish to be pilloried for interrogating a sick woman. You say she's not sick. Right. Then you say—'

'What I say is, she's still apparently oblivious.'

'Apparently—yes. So I ask her questions to find out, and everyone jumps down my throat.' Huffing away to a sideboard, Mossop swung about and leaned on it with both elbows, regarding with animosity the hunched figure in the chair before the stove.

'I take it,' Larkin said with diffidence, 'they were fair questions?'

'Far from it,' Mrs Thorpe averred.

The chief inspector wagged a finger. 'Listen here, Larkin. You're in no position to strike attitudes. Let me remind you . . . Well, we needn't go into that. But you stick to your sphere and I'll stumble along in mine, oafish and clumsy though I may be. What I shan't tolerate is being dictated to by members of the public. There's nothing—'

Sergeant Willis's head came round the door. 'Call for you, sir.'

With a final glare, Mossop marched out. Mrs Thorpe resumed at once.

'So I thought the best thing was to get you over here, Mr Larkin—and thank you very much for coming—to let that man see for himself that Hilda doesn't know you. Now he's gone away.' She looked across at Willis who had remained at the door. 'You'll do. Watch this.'

She drew Larkin to the front of the chair. 'Look, dear,' she implored her sister. 'Look who's come to see you.'

Hilda looked up. And smiled.

'Hullo, Mr Larkin.'

Irene gasped. The sergeant stiffened. Mrs Thorpe gazed down at her sister, her jaw hanging slightly.

'You do know him, dear?'

'Mr Larkin—I heard you call him that.' Hilda's voice was quavery but composed.

'Well yes. I did. I didn't think you were taking any—'

'All talking so loudly,' said Hilda with petulance. 'Standing around me . . . move away,' she added suddenly, twisting in the chair. Irene retreated nervously. Hilda renewed the smile. 'Will you be staying long, Mr Larkin?'

With a glance at her sister he leaned towards her. 'A few days,' he said clearly. 'I'm hoping to get a room at the Stag . . .'

'Rather cramped here,' she said as though he hadn't spoken. 'Only a small place as you can see.'

'Don't worry. How many rooms has the Stag?'

'But we keep nice and warm. Nothing like a fire, I always say.' She smoothed the housecoat across her knees. The room was silent.

'I was wondering about the Stag,' said Larkin. 'Shall I find the Sandersons there? Mr and Mrs Sanderson, or Maisie?'

Slowly her head came up. He held his breath.

The door opened smartly, hurling Willis across the room. Mossop marched back. 'If you've finished your chat,' he said loudly, 'I'd like you to come back to the station with me, Larkin, if you'd be so kind.'

On the return journey Irene was pensive. Half-way back she said, 'He's right about himself, that Mossop. He's disastrously clumsy. What d'you think about Hilda?'

'Shock of some kind.'

'She's closed her mind to anything connected with the Stag. What could she have seen?'

'Or is it bluff?' he asked.

'If so, she's certainly keeping it up.'

'She'd have to, assuming it was something she and they had worked out together.' He cleared his throat. 'Irene, I think I ought to square with you. Do you know why Mossop's coming back?'

'Something to do with the call he had?'

'Unless I'm mistaken, it was to tell him that Smut had called at headquarters with some information.'

'About the Sandersons?'

'Concerning the Royal.'

He was still telling her when he pulled up behind Smut's Volkswagen outside the station. She sat dumbly, taking it in, while the following patrol car slid in behind and disgorged its passenger. Larkin said, 'That's it in a nutshell,' and climbed out to join him. They hurried inside.

Larkin waited in the tiny bare outer room until he was summoned. Smut threw him a welcoming grimace. Without preamble Mossop said, 'Is this what you were going to tell us this afternoon?'

'Had you let me.'

'I suppose you think you've been smart?'

'Not in the least, quite the contrary. And I don't feel you were especially acute either.'

'We needn't descend,' said Mossop dangerously, 'to personal abuse.'

'Agreed.'

'You're not out of the wood yet, not by many a mile. Even if we find them, I'm still going to take some convincing that you weren't involved yourself.'

'If you find them you can ask them, can't you?'

'I wouldn't believe a word out of any of you,' growled the chief inspector. 'Stay here.' He went out, thumping the door.

'I was delayed,' said Smut apologetically. 'After you ejected I motored back into town, then suddenly noticed this car on my tail. As a test I drove home: sure enough there he was, parked along the road. Carrie knew what to do.'

'What?'

'She stormed along and confronted him. He was a cop all right—seconded from Lifton—and he was meant to be keeping tabs on a certain J. Larkin . . .'

'Then why was he chasing you?'

'He'd watched us both leave the Royal and get into my wagon. Drove behind us to where we parked and nattered; failed to see you get out to stroll back. Dozy bastard.'

'So he went on tailing your car?'

'Correct. By the time we'd sorted him out and he'd taken off in a frenzy to pick up your trail, it was half an hour before I finally got here. To find Mossop away. Where's he been? Oh, the Cotteridge dame. So I spilled my yarn—your yarn—to his deputy idiot, name of Hopper, likewise fresh to the district, who said it would be investigated, sir, in due course of time, and tried to nudge me out of the shop. Eventually I managed to persuade him this might just be something more than wild surmise based on malicious rumour, and got him to contact the chief. This explains,' said Smut, inhaling a large breath, 'the snail's-pace development of events, and also why you were able to parade about unencumbered. Or weren't you?'

Larkin explained briefly what had occurred. 'Hilda's pretty obviously still in shock.'

'Yeah. The shock of trying to drown herself.'

'Middle-aged spinsters,' Larkin concurred, 'are notorious for their over-reactions.' He reflected a moment. 'I don't know. Mossop's far from convinced she's not play-acting.'

'Still a guard on her at the cottage?'

'A supervisory attendance,' corrected Larkin. 'I hardly think Mossop will relax in any direction. He's taking—'

The subject of his remarks reappeared in a bustle.

'Smut—your sister-in-law works at the Royal, right? She can tell us the earliest time we could pay the place a visit without half Fleet Street being up and around to watch us?'

'I can tell you that,' grinned Smut. 'Twenty minutes after the bar shuts. But she's outside, why not ask her?'

'Turned eleven-thirty,' Mossop observed, leading the way. 'If we could arrive discreetly—'

He halted on the footway. The three of them looked at the empty space between Smut's Volkswagen and the patrol car. Mossop gestured. 'Didn't you leave your car there, Mr Larkin?'

'I did.' He glanced at Smut. 'With Irene inside it.'

CHAPTER XVI

MICHAEL MET THEM in the foyer.

'Good evening, Chief Inspector. What's this, a raid or a social call? We don't serve drinks after hours, you know.'

Mossop steered him aside. Smut and Larkin took seats on the bay next to the entrance; the three young constables stood stiffly around the foyer, studying the grain of the wall-panelling. Detective-Inspector Hopper and another constable had gone to the rear car park.

The hotel was silent. Half the lights, including those in the bar, had been switched off. The hunch-backed porter, who had opened the door to them, lurked in the shadow of the reception desk. The clock above it struck a quarter to twelve.

'Daft little muddlehead,' Smut muttered, partly to himself. 'Wait till I see her.'

Larkin said nothing.

Signing to two of the constables to follow, Mossop set off with Michael for the stairs. The four of them plodded upwards out of sight. Smut moved restlessly.

'Where d'you reckon she is now?'

'My fault,' said Larkin. 'I shouldn't have told her.'

'Home with her folks, I guess. Having blown the gaff.'

'It may not have made any difference.'

'Put it any way you like,' said Irene's brother-in-law, 'it can't have helped.'

Minutes elapsed.

From the shadows the porter observed them covertly,

like a timorous Morlock. The foyer grew chiller. Or else, thought Larkin, he himself was shedding body heat built up by the pace of events, along with the lassitude that earlier had threatened to swallow him. Mentally he was more alert than ever. He felt ready for a five-hour game of chess. A pipe would have helped. He was out of tobacco, and in any case had left his matches in the car. Smut vented a vast yawn.

'Lucky I told Carrie I might be late.'

'Tomorrow's your press day,' Larkin remarked.

'Bloody nearly today.' Smut compared his watch with the clock.

'I only hope you get something to make it worthwhile.'

'Won't be your fault if I don't.'

'Fleet Street seems satisfyingly recumbent.'

'Take an earth tremor to shift that lot,' Smut said scornfully. 'Nocturnally, that is. What's that cretin doing up there?'

His words reached the remaining constable, who regarded him stonily. Smut flapped an arm. 'Sorry, Ken. Merely voicing impatience. Don't you feel they ought to be through by now?'

The young officer made a quarter-turn in the other direction. Smut quirked his mouth at Larkin. 'Starchily on duty, and very proper too. A far cry from—'

The reception telephone rang. Everyone jumped. The porter clutched the instrument to an ear.

'She en't here,' he told it. 'She bin gorn some while, Mrs Matthews. Naw, she en't—'

'Irene's mum.' Smut jumped up and went to the desk. 'Mind if I speak to her?' Thankfully the porter yielded the phone. The constable watched indecisively. 'Hullo, Mam, this is Frankie. Never mind what I'm doing here: you were asking about Irene? She's not come in? I can't tell you where she is, but I can tell you not to worry: it's just a rather odd—What? Well, it's to do with that in a way, but only indirectly. I mean she's not in any danger. Actually I'm a bit narked with her. I'll explain later. Look, Mam, you hop off to bed, the two of you, and stop fretting, all right? She'll be home quite soon. Yes, a promise. Yes. We'll be round. 'Night, then.'

Contemplatively Smut hung up. He looked across at Larkin, and as an afterthought at the constable. 'Irene hasn't—'

Mossop descended the stairs and walked over briskly. 'Who was that?'

'My mother-in-law. Asking about my sister-in-law.'

'Don't tell me *she*'s missing,' said the chief inspector tiredly.

'She's not reached home yet,' Smut admitted, 'but that's hardly remarkable, is it?' He sent a glance to the foot of the staircase, where Michael and the two constables had arrived. 'What news?'

Mossop spoke in a monotone.

'We've been given every facility by Mr Potter. No trace was found to suggest recent occupancy by any of the parties we're concerned with. Or anyone at all.'

'There could have been a warning—'

'Mr Potter has satisfied me entirely that no further search is warranted.' Mossop's eyes slid to brush Larkin's. 'The attic floor of this establishment is empty, unfurnished, and heavily infested with rodents.' He glanced back at Potter. 'A visit from the public health inspector may be in the offing, but he's seen the last of us.'

Larkin rose.

'Chief Inspector,' he said urgently. 'With the **advance** notice there may have been, isn't it possible—'

'Nobody's lived up there for five days. Not for five hours. There's dust an inch thick, paw-marks where the hotel cat's been having a go, and several plates of rodent poison—put down, I understand, by the head waiter.' Mossop restored his attention to Smut. 'They're super-mice, it seems. Resistant to most of the stuff available. Now Mr Potter's resorted to cyanide bait. Naturally he had to seal off the floor.' He subjected Larkin to a final corrosive scrutiny. 'I'll want another word with you in the morning.' Gathering his constables about him, he left.

Michael advanced.

'No doubt with the best intentions,' he said politely to Larkin, 'you've landed us in a spot of trouble, I'm afraid.'

Smut spoke bluntly. 'Jim merely reported what he'd seen and heard. If you'd been less secretive about it—'

'We had to be,' Michael said quickly. 'Had it got known that we were infested, we could have been closed down till the little beggars were got rid of. Just when we were in demand. Dad left it to me, and I got old Vic to put down the bait. Irene told me, Mr Larkin, you'd complained of hearing thumps, but by that time we were fully booked and I couldn't transfer you.'

'They were loud thumps,' Larkin said coldly.

Michael nodded. 'I've heard them myself. They're nesting under the floorboards; the noise you hear is them jumping down on to the plasterboard. Makes quite a racket. We're not alone in this,' he added defensively. 'Mice are a real problem around here. They've had similar trouble at the Stag.'

'You should import a few cats.'

'I think that's what I may do. We had old Smokey up there a couple of nights, but he couldn't cope. He's a poor mouser.'

Smut said sceptically, 'You kept all this from Irene?'

'Oh definitely. None of the staff knew, except Vic. We simply shut off the whole floor. When Irene shot in tonight and told me what was suspected, I was aghast.'

'She's still here, I suppose?' inquired Smut.

'Here?' Michael's forehead creased. 'Not to my knowledge. She said she was off home.'

'How long ago's that?'

'Quite a while. She came in about eleven-fifteen, told me what she'd heard and then left. There's nowhere here for her.'

'Why isn't she home, then?'

'Isn't she?'

'Not according to her mum. It's only ten minutes' walk from here, for Christ's sake. Jim—you're sure that was your MG parked at the back?'

'No question. And she'd left the keys.'

'I reckon,' said Smut ominously, 'she's whipped it again while we've been in here. And gone off to spend the night with one of her chums.'

'Would she do that without notifying her parents?'

Smut shook his head. 'I'll give 'em a buzz, see if she's back.'

Michael said to Larkin, 'Did Irene borrow your car?'

'In a manner of speaking.'

Something tugged at the younger Potter's mouth. Gazing at Smut on the telephone, he appeared to calculate. At last he said, 'She left it here at the back? Then she couldn't have taken it again. The chief inspector had men posted there.'

'They'll be gone by now.'

Smut said, 'Righto, Mam, leave it with me.' He dropped the receiver. The porter patted it into place.

'Think you know where she is?' asked Larkin.

Smut was frowning. 'Her friend Doreen, I'll lay any odds—but why didn't she tell her folks? You know what: she's uptight about what she did, so she panicked. I'll have to go and dig her out. Christ, what a night.'

'Can't you ring?'

'Doreen's not on the phone, blast her. No need for you to worry, Jim. It's only a few minutes in the car.'

Larkin turned to Michael. 'You may prefer that I find somewhere else to sleep for the—'

'We wouldn't be so petty, Mr Larkin. You thought you were acting for the best. You're most welcome to stay on.'

'Thank you,' he said with difficulty.

'I'll say good night if you don't mind. A hectic day tomorrow,' Michael smiled, 'coping with our London guests, and no doubt also with a caller from the public health department.' The smile blistered Larkin's face and was carried off.

CHAPTER XVII

'WELL,' said Larkin, 'there it is.'

He walked over to the MG, parked where Irene had left it between Ian Butler's Jaguar and a wall. 'Keys here still,' he reported. 'So unless she took someone else's—'

'She'd have to have gone barmy,' said Smut. 'But then you can't tell with women. I'll get over to Doreen's right away.'

Larkin leaned back against the car and stared skywards.

'I'm still unsatisfied.'

'As the chambermaid said to the bell-hop. Why, Jim?'

'To my mind, it's the only way it could have been done. Into the milkman's van that end, out at this, up that fire escape to the hideout. It all slots. Appleby wants to give his asthmatic daughter a holiday, he'd have done it for fifty quid. And when you think how the two hotels had been collaborating in their protests—'

'Sure, Jim, but you can't argue with an empty attic.'

'There was time to get them away.'

'Leaving no trace?'

'It could have been done. Must have been.'

'If you want my advice, which God forbid, you'll shove it out of your brain and go to bed. Otherwise,' said Smut, scowling at the face of his watch through the gloom, 'you're liable to find yourself locked out. Forget about today. You can't win 'em all.'

Having watched Smut's beetle out of sight, Larkin stood motionless at the car park entrance.

You can't win 'em all. But you can win the ones that count. His brain was racing: a return to his room, he knew, meant a dreary commitment to hours of sleeplessness, cerebral whirlpools. If he could just find a new slant . . .

Mossop had seemed convinced. All right; there were mice. Very convenient. How much noise could the creatures make? *As quiet as a mouse.* But dozens of them? Plasterboard . . .

His attention switched to the street.

Something had jogged his eyesight. The instant his brain took notice, the thing was gone; nothing was to be seen. Between dark buildings lay lamplit pools of road. No vehicle was in sight, no other light, no movement. No other light. Quitting the entrance, he walked slowly and quietly along the bitumined footpath towards the Stag.

Halting opposite, he studied the inn.

Its frontal stonework threw back faint radiance from a street lamp to his right; the windows were pale facsimiles of the sodium glow, like square anaemic flames in sunlight. His gaze travelled from one to the next. The strongest reflections came from the downstairs panes. On the ground floor, all the curtains were drawn across.

Suddenly he knew what it was he had seen.

He crossed the street. Testing with two fingers the porch door, he felt it yield, swing back with gathering momentum. He awaited the impact.

The door grounded, apparently on a mat. Its arrest was soundless. He glanced back. The street remained incuriously inert, folded in midnight coma, its façades coy and indistinct masses. He stepped into the porch.

Restoration of the door to its former position, into the frame but off the latch, left him in a blackness almost total. He felt for matches; and remembered. They were in the car.

He waited for his pupils to adjust. Presently he could see enough to enable him to ease through the revolving door with a minimum of disturbance. Inside, he paused again.

He tried to recall the geography. The exercise helped to flatten the lifting hairs on his neck, but achieved little else. In front of him, the counter; to his half-left, the stairs; to his left, the lounge door. On relative distances he was hazy. The sensible thing, he informed himself, was to return to the street, find a telephone, contact Mossop and tell him he had seen a curtain move behind a ground-floor window of the Stag and that the street door was ajar.

'Larkin, did you say? I want to see you in the morning, don't forget.'

'But there are people inside the Stag.'

'Well, that makes a nice change. I'll talk to them in daylight.'

'By then they'll have done what they want.'

'What? Put out poison for the rats?'

'They'll have moved back. Can't you see? As though nothing had ever happened, as if they'd never been away. The Lost Five Days. Story of the month. Whereas if you catch them now, resettling themselves in, they'll look stupid.'

'Talking of stupidity, Larkin . . .'

In the darkness he realized that one side of his mouth had set in an obstinate rigidity. He relaxed the muscles: but stubbornly, from habit, he moved forward.

High in the street wall of the foyer, a porthole-sized window admitted light in derisory driblets, subtracting marginally from the Stygian murk but adding nothing of its own. The lounge door must be directly ahead.

The knuckles of his groping right hand rapped wood and glass. Opening the door, he went through.

His eyes were beginning to combat the gloom's intensity. Outlines of the inglenook, the seats and tables, toiled into his retinal compass. Despite this he cannoned into a drinks trolley that was parked, he remembered instantly, to the right of the door, sending it trundling into a corner where it was brought resoundingly to a stop, its cargo of glasses composing a tinkling serenade of a volume surpassed by its dissonance.

Frozen where he stood, he counted to sixty.

Nothing happened. Nothing, he reminded himself, had happened since his entry. No sound, no movement: only what he had produced himself. 'Something of a busybody, aren't we, Larkin? Now about this previous conviction of ours . . .'

In exasperation, partly self-directed, he clawed around for a light switch. Further caution seemed pointless. An old-fashioned protrusion met his fingers; he pressed it down. The room remained dark.

Which settled things. Without light he could accomplish nothing: the call to Mossop would have to be made, whether he liked it or not, whether it achieved anything or not. He replaced his fingers on the door handle; and paused.

The thing that had caught his eye from outside the Royal was a curtain movement. And yet from that distance he couldn't actually have seen the curtain. What he had seen was the dart of radiance before the curtain was replaced. Therefore . . .

Turning again, he advanced slowly, guiding himself between tables, past the inglenook, into the passage that led to the dining-room. On his right lay the kitchen door. Its precise position he couldn't recall. Holding a palm against the rough brick wall, a continuation of the inglenook, he slid it as he paced along. A dry, rasping sound came from his fingertips. Like rapid human breaths. So powerful was the resemblance that he suspended movement to listen.

The stealthy panting continued.

Imaginative as he was, Larkin possessed in strong measure the capacity to override imagery, to keep a clinical eye on fundamentals. The facility now deserted him. Striking out blindly with both hands, he scrabbled the wall, felt a nail tear, encountered brick and mortar in a frustrating expanse. Sidestepping twice, he found timber. Momentum brought him against it heavily: it yielded, so that his body went on. His leading foot searched vainly for a landing place. He was falling.

The breath was knocked out of him. He lay with chin and hands resting on something cold and hard. Slowly he identified it as the tiled floor of the kitchen.

Lifting himself, he heard his own efforts to reinflate his lungs, a laboured inhalation that seemed to fill the room. Remembering, he dragged himself backwards. A contact with his shoulder-blades produced a metallic boom: an oven, or the freezer. In the pitch blackness he struggled up.

'Someone here,' he said loudly. 'Who is it?'

Nearby, a tiny movement was perceptible. His voice sounded high, insecure. 'Jim Larkin's my name. I came in because the street door was ajar. Tell me who you are.'

A new sound intruded. Like the opening of a cupboard door. He moved to his left. Soft noises; as though a creature were dabbing with a paw.

Light exploded in his eyes.

Blinking painfully, he stared across the kitchen at the person who was looking at him. It was Hilda Cotteridge.

CHAPTER XVIII

'Why hilda,' he said gently, 'how did you get here?'

Her middle finger was still on the switch inside the mains cupboard. She stood beside it in a huddled attitude, as though waiting contritely for admonishment.

'What are you doing?' he asked.

She seemed to stiffen, to gain in stature.

'Came to see everything was all right.'

'Well of course it is. The police have been looking after the place. You needn't have worried.'

She was still wrapped in the housecoat she had worn at the cottage; her feet were slippered. Wispy gunmetal hair hung each side of the corroded face: her eyes were the centre of blackened circles, with puckers of skin beneath. They were looking his way, but not meeting his own.

He added, 'You shouldn't be here, you know. You're not well enough.'

He took a step towards her. She shrank.

'What will your sister think? She'll be anxious.'

Like a rebellious girl she shook her head. Her hand left the cupboard to hang at her side like the other, completing the first-former effect. He went a step closer.

'Don't you think I should phone her, tell her you're here?'

Hilda said, 'She's asleep.'

'Sergeant Willis is there. Won't he answer?'

She gazed at him dumbly. He leaned against the stainless steel sink, arms folded in a casual manner.

'I'd still like to know how you got here. Did you borrow your sister's car?' She nodded.

'Well,' he said agreeably, 'I think it might be a good thing if you now drove yourself back.' In reaction, his heart was pounding his ribs. 'I'll come too, if you like. You've had a look around, seen that everything's okay. That's what you wanted, isn't it?'

'I've got the keys,' she told the sink unit. 'Always had the keys.'

'They trust you, don't they, Hilda? Shall I phone your sister now?'

'Came to see everything's all right.'

He said reasonably, 'There's no one here at present, you know. No guests. Not until the Sandersons get back. Do you know when that is?'

She kept her gaze on the unit.

'I thought you might have known that, Hilda. I thought they might have told you, since they trust you. But it doesn't matter. When they do come back, you'll be able to return to work. That's what you enjoy, isn't it?'

Her gaze shifted across the kitchen. Settled upon a powered tin-opener fixed to a wall.

'Let's hope it's not too long. If it is, the inn might have to close. You might never get the visitors here again.'

He watched her intently.

'And you wouldn't like that.'

Her body stirred. 'I've got the keys.'

'Yes, but it needs the four of you. Mr and Mrs Sanderson, Maisie and yourself. All looking after the guests. I wanted to stay here, you know. I couldn't, because you'd all gone.'

She shivered, and looked into his eyes. He moved forward. 'Let me run you home.'

Ducking away, she scuttled across the tiles to take up a new station beside the freezer.

'Not going home,' she said.

'You'll be here all alone.'

Presently he added briskly, 'All right, Hilda. I'll go back to the Royal, leave you in peace. You can have the Stag to yourself.' He glanced at the mains cupboard. 'You'll need warmth. Is the central heating worked from—'

As he started towards the cupboard she moved to block the way. He stopped.

'You know how it operates, of course. No one knows as much about this place as you do.'

She said, '*They* know I'm to be trusted.'

'Everyone knows that. So I'll be off, leave you to your work. A lot to be done, isn't there?'

She looked past him. He followed her gaze. 'What's kept in there, as a rule?'

Turning, he strode over to the freezer. The door opened with a clunk, releasing a smell of mildew. Except for two packets of peas the interior was empty. He glanced back. She was watching vacantly.

'Of course,' he remarked, 'the power's been off. Now it's on again—eh, Hilda? All back to normal. What else did they tell you to do?'

He went back to confront her. 'Air the beds? Prepare food? You're a smart woman, Hilda. I guarantee you'll think of everything, have it shipshape again in the blink of an eye while your sister covers up for you back home. You'll handle it, won't you, Hilda? As arranged.'

Her heavy shoulders sagged. The housecoat was slack at her throat, her neck compressed. He moved a hand in front of her eyes.

'Listening, Hilda? You faked that jump into the stream, didn't you? The rescue was allowed for?'

She stood as though cataleptic. He gripped her arms.

'All to add to the mystery . . . and you were simply following orders. I don't blame you, Hilda. You were worried about the inn. They persuaded you it was a good plan. Is that how it was?' He shook her slightly. 'No one's condemning you in this. You were misguided. Anyone with an ounce of—'

He stopped.

Above the resonance of his own voice a sound had reached him. A low-pitched cry.

Releasing Hilda, he went to the door. It had closed itself. Reopening it, he mounted the step into the passage, took a swift look at the now illuminated dining-room, returned to the lounge. There was nothing to be seen. Continuing into the foyer, he made for the stairs.

The cry came again. From behind him, it seemed. He ran back into the lounge. Muffled movements were audible. He thought of rodents. Pursuing the sounds, he came to the inglenook and stood still. Now there was silence.

'Is anybody—'

'Please help me!' The call, muffled and yet startlingly close, cut into his words. It came from behind the brickwork. The voice was a girl's, sharpened by pure horror. At that instant the lights went out.

'Hilda!' His own voice was a shout. 'Put the lights on again at once!'

From the kitchen came a clatter, a scuttle of footsteps. He said loudly, 'Just a moment—there's help coming,' and groped his way to the left. This time he could judge the distance. Kicking open the kitchen door he stepped down, hands raised protectively. They met nothing. He took tentative steps to where he calculated the mains cupboard to be.

A corner hit the back of his outstretched hand. The door had been closed. Wrenching it back, he felt for the switch.

Banks of dials, smooth rounded surfaces answered his touch. He tried to the right, found a lever, tugged it down. Nothing happened. He worked back, investigating each dial. His thumb and forefinger traced a square outline, a projection; he snapped it down. Light engulfed him.

The kitchen was empty. Making his way back, he called sharply, 'Hilda? Where are you hiding?'

Someone had blocked the passage. Where previously it had led into the lounge, a wall now faced him. The sight brought him to a standstill. He saw that he could still get through. Pushing into the gap, he felt the brickwork sway and swing in his grasp.

Where it had been was now an oblong hole beside the inglenook. On the floor in front of it lay a girl. She was sprawled with her face to the carpet, arms outflung. Kneeling, he turned her cautiously and looked at the face of Irene.

Working an arm beneath her, he braced himself to lift her away. In doing so he looked into the cavity.

The room lights gave partial vision. He saw crates, one on top of another, piled high. At the foot of them were shapes. Gently lowering Irene, he crawled nearer.

Now he could see better: they were people, three of

them, reclining against the crates. They were looking at him.

He said breathlessly, 'Are you all right? Let me help you out . . .'

Then he saw that they were dead.

CHAPTER XIX

Behind him there was a laugh.

Without turning he said quietly, 'Come here, please, Hilda, and help. We've work to do.'

No reply. Slowly he turned to look.

She was kneeling on the far side of Irene's prostrate figure, the aftermath of the laugh still on her lips. The length of copper piping clutched in her right hand was aimed at the girl's temple. She was staring at him.

He stayed in a crouch. In the same low-key voice he said, 'So, Hilda, you had us all fooled. You knew where they were and we didn't.'

She said in a pleased way, '*I* knew they were there.'

'How could you guess, if we couldn't?'

'Didn't have to guess.' The smile lifted from her teeth. 'I knew.'

'Because you put them there?'

'I put them there.' Nodding complacently, she ducked her head a little to peer past him into the hole. The copper piping quivered in her grasp.

'Why did you do that, Hilda?'

For a while he got no answer. She knelt immobile, humming breathily to herself. She seemed to forget his question. He was about to speak again when the humming stopped.

'Lose her again,' she crooned. 'Didn't want that. Lose my little girl again.'

'So you put her in there—with them?'

'My little Sarah. I wanted to keep her. It was the

155

only place,' she explained to him lucidly, as though no one could possibly misunderstand.

Again she ducked her head to gaze beyond him. 'Doesn't she look beautiful? She's so lovely. *They* weren't going to have her.' Her voice changed, became harsh. 'They tried but I got the better of them. I saw to it.'

'You're clever, Hilda. What did you do?'

Her pupils went opaque. The piping hung slack in her fingers. He measured the distance. Hilda stirred. 'The rats,' she said clearly.

'Rats?'

'Get rid of them, *she* said. Can't have rats here, not nice. I told her. Years past, I said, *we* never cared about rats, they never hindered us, we let them be. You get rid of them, she says, and she gives me the stuff. Poison, it said on the jar.'

'What did you do with it, Hilda?'

'Fetch the sherry in, Hilda, she says. We'll have it here, she says, here in the lounge—we're celebrating. Pour it out for us, Hilda. We're celebrating the adoption. No, no, I wasn't having that.'

'The adoption? Tell me about it, Hilda, I'm very interested.'

'Four sherries to celebrate. Three pills out of the jar. One each for them, one for my Sarah.'

'What were the pills?'

Her eyes crossed slightly as she seemed to consult a mental index.

'I see what it says. On the label. Cyanide of potassium, it says. Use under strict control.' She giggled suddenly. 'One each. Never took long.'

Larkin glanced into the cavity.

'So no one else could have her,' he said softly.

'Sitting there, holding their glasses. Cheers, every-body, good luck. Come on, Hilda, drink to the occasion. So I drink. More sherry? I asks them. Only they never answer. So I drags them inside. Them two first, her last. Never took long.'

'Fine place to keep her, Hilda.'

'Made her comfy, I did. Saw to it she was comfy.'

'Nobody else knew of it. How was that?'

'Mr Barrett, he knows.'

'The Barretts have gone, Hilda.'

'He'll not let on.'

'So it was Mr Barrett who installed this place?'

'Plenty of room, there is.' She was talking wholly to herself, staring down at the piping in her hand. 'Keep her happy. Happy and comfy, my Sarah. *They* wasn't having her. Not them two. She belongs to me. You hear?' She glared around the lounge. 'No one takes her off. She stays here where she belongs. You hear me?'

'I hear you, Hilda,' he said gravely. 'We won't touch them. But will you give me a hand with Irene? I want her carried over there, on to the padded seat. And then I want you to find me some brandy. You'll do that for me, won't you?'

On hands and knees, he was moving back to Irene's side when a quick movement of Hilda's body told him, too late, that he had miscalculated.

The pain connected neck with brain in a single pulsing ache. It dominated all else. Bringing up his forces, he set out to fight, to sever the connection, feel it snap. A voice called.

Answering it was too arduous by far. He concentrated on the struggle. Soon the priorities blurred. His body rocked. Something was shaking it, adding ruthlessly to the pain. He resisted. He opened his eyes, but saw nothing.

'Jim! Answer me, please . . .'

'I'm awake,' he mumbled into the darkness.

'Oh thank Heaven!' Irene sobbed on his chest.

He moved both legs. His feet kicked something that didn't yield, jarring him, sending waves of agony into his skull. 'Where the devil are we?'

'She's shut us in.' He felt the shuddering of Irene's body. 'She's mad, Jim.'

'I won't dispute that.' He experimented with a sitting posture: immediately a host of small cranial hammers surged into action. He groaned. Irene let out a gasp.

'What is it?' he demanded.

'I thought . . .' He felt her taking breaths, steadying herself. 'Hilda's gone,' she said lifelessly.

'Maybe not. I think she'll probably stick around. Know anything about this place?'

'Only that I want to get out.'

So complete was the blackness that it was like sitting with bandaged eyes; their voices seemed to boom across deep space. Moving with caution, Larkin groped at the walls. They were solid. Pulling himself groggily to his feet, he tried higher.

'Nothing to get hold of,' he reported. 'Door must fit to a millimetre. And it's worked from a switch in the kitchen. So we'll have to wait.' He slid down beside her.

'Wait?'

'Till someone comes. They'll hear us calling. I heard you.'

'Jim.' Her voice betrayed hysteria. 'I can't. Not here.'

'It's just a storeroom.'

'But they're all—'

'No,' he said quickly. 'She moved them out first.'

He couldn't tell whether she believed him. Finding his right hand with both of hers, she clung tight. He guided her back to lean against the invisible brickwork. The chill of the stone floor climbed into them.

To divert her mind he added, 'What happened to you at the police station?'

After an interval she found her voice again. 'I drove back in your car to warn Mike. Sorry, Jim. I felt I had to.'

'Think nothing of it. But how did you get here?'

'When I left the hotel to walk home I saw this car go by and turn into the Stag entrance. I thought that was f-funny, so I stood and watched.'

'Recognize the car?'

'Mrs Thorpe's Escort. It has an odd note to the engine.' Irene's voice gained strength. 'I thought, what's she doing here this time of night? Then I saw this figure come back to the porch and let herself in . . .'

'You could see it was Hilda?'

'I know the way she walks, with a stoop.'

'What did you do then?'

'Walked along and stood outside, wondering if I should tell anyone. I was sure she shouldn't be there. We'd only left her an hour before at her sister's place. How d'you think she got out, Jim?'

'I'm trying not to think,' he said grimly. 'She'd left the porch door ajar?'

'It was shut, but the latch hadn't gone back in. The door's warped or something. I opened it and put my head round, but I couldn't see Hilda though the lights were all on. I went through into the foyer—'

'Weren't you scared?'

'Petrified. It was only because I knew it was Hilda . . . I was looking through the lounge door when I heard this grinding noise and a sort of rumble. I thought the place was collapsing. Then I saw the wall by the fireplace moving. Swinging out. I tried to run but I couldn't . . .'

Irene's hand was damp. He pulled her closer. 'Carry on, tell me everything. What about Hilda?'

'She came in from the kitchen. There was this weird look in her eyes. She saw me standing there and came over, opened the door and grabbed me. I couldn't move. She pulled me into the lounge. She's so strong. I managed to get free and make a dash for a window, but I'd only just pulled the curtain back when she caught me again. I was so terrified, I lost my voice.'

'Did she hit you?'

'No. Just dragged me over here. I could see inside and—and there they were, looking at me. I don't remember any more. I must have passed out.'

'And when you came round,' Larkin said in a normal voice, 'here you were.'

'It was so dark. I called out: then I heard you shouting to Hilda. Somehow I thought we were at the Royal and there'd been a power failure. Then there was more rumbling and the wall began to open—'

'That was me. I threw the switch in the kitchen by mistake.'

'The light came in and I saw them again—right next to me. I don't know what I did. I must have flung myself out and fainted again. That's all I remember until—'

'Until a blundering half-wit called Larkin contrived to get us both incarcerated.' He gave her a rallying

160

squeeze. 'Not so bright, but things could be darker. Someone will be along soon.'

'You think so?' Hope filtered into her voice. 'How about air?'

'Plenty to go on with.'

She relaxed slightly. Their joint breathing became noticeable in the blackness. To counter its hypnotic effect, Larkin began talking again.

'What's all this about Sarah?'

'Sarah? What do you mean?'

'Hilda seemed to be calling Maisie that. Telling me she was hers. Mean anything to you?'

There was silence. At last Irene said, 'There's supposed to have been an affair at one time between Hilda and a local man. They say she had a baby. The father wouldn't marry her, and she was persuaded to give the child away. That's the story. Mum's told me about it. But it would have been a long time ago.'

'How long?'

'Before I was born. Thirty years at least.'

Larkin was silent, thinking.

'Jim? Keep talking.'

'Perhaps,' he suggested, 'we ought to conserve air. Just in case they're a little longer than I expect in finding us.'

CHAPTER XX

HE AWOKE from a cramped doze to find Irene's body across his stomach, her head resting in the crook of his left arm. His cautious movements roused her.

'What time is it, Jim?'

'No idea. Watch-hands aren't luminous.' He put an ear to his wrist. 'Stopped anyhow.'

'D'you think it's light outside?'

'Hope so.'

'My watch is going,' she said. 'I can hear the tick. Haven't you a match?'

'As an inveterate pipe-smoker,' he told her, 'I'm chastened to say I left them in the car. I deserve to be drummed out of the Puffers' League.'

He felt a shiver run through her. 'Cold?' he asked.

'And scared. I never thought I could feel so scared.'

'Think of it as a night's camping. Were you in the Guides?'

'I used to run the company. Mellaby Forest was never like this.'

'From my experience,' he remarked, 'tents are a lot damper. Any canvas I was under seemed to have fed the moth population for years. Do you hear a noise?'

They were both silent, listening.

'Can't hear anything. What did it sound like?'

'Thuds.'

'You're always hearing them.' She laughed with a return of the hysteria. Then she sniffed once or twice and seemed to be thinking. 'Did they search the Royal? Did they find anything?'

He told her. He spoke sparingly, because the air was getting stale. Also he wanted to listen. For a while he heard nothing; he decided it had been noises in his own head. He was describing in comic terms Michael's reaction to the police invasion when he paused: by her silence he knew that she had heard it too.

'They're looking for us,' she said excitedly.

Larkin raised his voice. 'Hullo there! We're behind the wall, next to the chimney . . .'

Nobody answered. Presently the faint thudding resumed. Irene said doubtfully, 'It's coming from the kitchen.'

'Let's shout again.'

They called in unison. In the confined space the result was deafening. He said, 'The wall must muffle it a lot.'

'Jim, I've had a thought. What about the back?'

'The back?'

'Where would this place butt on to?'

With his unreliable mental map he tried to work it out. 'Somewhere between kitchen and staircase, is my guess.'

'If it's the kitchen, the partition may be quite thin or there might be a connecting hatch. We could knock a way through.'

'Best to sit tight,' he said, 'and wait to be found.'

'Why?'

'Exertion means using up air.'

'I can't sit here much longer, Jim.'

'Do your best.'

'I'm starting to feel panicky.'

'Why don't we play a game? I'll ask you for a word meaning—'

'Wouldn't do any good. Let's try and get out, Jim.'

'All right,' he said after a pause. 'Stay here, don't budge. I'll shift a few crates and test the wall that side . . . if I can without breaking an arm. I'm leaving go of you—okay?'

'Okay.' Her voice trembled.

He crawled away from her. The darkness beat in with almost a physical sensation on his face. His hand came down on something soft: with a shudder he snatched it away, made a detour to his left. His shoulder struck a hard edge, producing a clash of bottles.

Reaching out, he traced the outline of the stack, felt for the top crate, lifted it down. Depositing it behind him, he added others to it, working down to floor level. He wormed into the gap.

'Smoother surface here,' he said across his shoulder.

'Think it's as thick?'

'Hard to say.' He rapped it with a fist. 'Sounds solid.'

'Hit it with a crate.'

'Just what I intend to do.' Twisting, he began removing bottles from the crate nearest him. His ears picked up the sound of tearing cobwebs. If spiders, he reasoned, could find a way in, there must be cracks. Or did the creatures breed out of nothing, spontaneous products of a fusion of elements born of dirt and darkness? Or had their eggs been brought in with the stores? The crate was empty. Picking it up, he weighed it in both hands.

'This is going to make a noise.'

'Good,' she said violently.

'Stand by. I'm hitting . . . now.'

The shock of impact swept up his arms, recharging the throb at the base of his skull. Recoiling, he fell backwards on to a shape that shifted under him. His appalled grunt was only half stifled.

'Jim—what have you done? Are you all right?'

He dragged himself clear. 'Fine. Just struck with . . . rather too much enthusiasm.' Nausea lurked. Swallowing hard, he retrieved the crate. 'Try again.'

Repeatedly he attacked the wall, panting as the effort mounted. At last he dropped the crate. 'Useless. It's making no impression.'

'Let me try.'

'Stay where you are, Irene.' He was too late. He heard the scuffling as she came away from the other wall, the drag of her toes as she tried to find him. 'Over here.' He put out a hand.

'Sorry, Jim, I kicked you.'

'No, you didn't,' he said before he could help it.

There was a brief silence. Then he heard the intake of breath that preceded the choking scream that came from her. Kneeling his way across, he wrapped her in his arms and lifted her back. She struggled, screaming again; he jerked her round, judged the direction as best he could and slapped her face. She stiffened, gave a gasping sob or two, went limp and was quiet. He held on to her.

She said weakly, 'All right now, Jim.'

He helped her sit down. 'They're just three nice people, Irene, who happen to be dead. They'll do us no harm.'

'No.' The syllable emerged on the tail of a gasp.

He spoke with forced briskness. 'That wall over there is as strong as this one—so we can rule it out. We'll sit here and wait for the doorman, and I'll drone an old Army song or two, just to see if they shock you. Ready?'

'Yes,' she said obediently. She leaned into him like a child.

Towards the end of the fifth song the new sound came to them.

He stopped in mid-phrase. The sound reminded him of something: heavy boots on dry twigs? He had a moment of hope.

'I believe I hear footsteps.'

Irene sat up. 'Help!' she called unsteadily.

He added his voice. When they listened again it was as though other feet had joined in to create a continuous crackling. 'What are they doing?' cried Irene. 'Can't they hear us?' She started to cough.

Acridity touched Larkin's nostrils. He leaned back, taking her with him, while his brain came to grips with the situation. Keeping his voice level, he said, 'Stay this side.'

'Something went down my throat . . .'

'Keep close to the floor.'

'What for? They might—' She stopped talking; he felt tension seize her muscles.

'Don't waste breath.'

'The air smells funny.'

'It's smoke,' he said, abandoning pretence. 'Hilda must have lit something in the fireplace and it's seeping through. Which means there are gaps. Now if we can take advantage—'

'The noise is getting worse,' she said with amazing calmness.

The crackling was subdued but distinct. Larkin pulled her down until both of them were lying flat, breathing air again, stale but absorbable. He strove to work out what to do and, just as vital, what to say.

Irene was no fool. As though to clinch the matter she forestalled him.

'It's as though it were all round us.'

She waited for him to deny it.

'Hilda's set fire to the place. Hasn't she?'

'I think so,' he said reluctantly. 'So it can't be long now. We'll have people here in no time.'

'But,' she said in a patient way, 'before they can get us out—'

He echoed her style of reasoned argument. 'The walls will keep the flames back.'

'But the smoke?'

'So long as we stay low.'

'The heat will build up.'

'You've just been complaining of the cold.'

'How d'you know the walls won't give way? Or the ceiling?'

'The ceiling,' he repeated.

'Stay down, Jim. Don't leave me.'

'You stay down. Keep there till I say.'

On his stomach, he felt around for the crates. Dragging four of them into a square, he added a second tier of two and topped off with a single. As his head reached smoke-level he began to choke. He dropped to draw breath.

She said, 'Is it high enough?'

'When my head hits the plaster, I'll let you know.'

Equipping himself with a spare empty crate, he inhaled to capacity and climbed the stack. It wobbled alarmingly, then resettled. Poised on the top crate, he straightened slowly: his right hand touched a surface that rang hollow to his knuckles.

Finding balance, he took the crate in both hands and jerked it upwards. He felt the give of the laths.

For a moment he held it there for support while the stack stopped rocking. Lowering it, he heaved again with all his force.

Plaster fell about him. His lungs were at bursting point. A third impact; a blow on the forehead as an area of plaster dropped away. His eyes were filled with powder. A splitting noise gave him heart: with the last of his strength he brought up the crate a fourth time, felt it sink into the latticed woodwork. Losing his hold, he fell sideways.

He tried to gauge his jump. The floor hit him sooner than expected. He lay gasping, coughing smoke from his chest.

'Jim, what's happened?'

'Get ready . . . follow me up. Wait for the word.'

Hoarding breath, he scrambled up again. The crate had remained lodged in the laths. After resistance it came free in a splintering of wood, a fresh shower of plaster. He threw it down, away from Irene; it landed softly, and a shudder ran through him.

No light entered by the hole he had made, but he felt a draught. Using it to snatch breath, he felt around, encountered the solid timber of a joist and, above it, floorboards.

Without hope, he battered at a board with the heel of his palm. Again his eyes were filled. Blinking away the dust, he attacked again, felt the wood disintegrate. Bless them, he thought, those beautiful little boring beasts. With renewed energy he hammered upwards. A section of board came away in his fingers: he hung upon the piece next to it, wrenching it away. Still no light.

'Climb up,' he shouted.

He heard her scrambling. Smoke was drifting about him, but the draught that travelled between floorboards and plaster kept the atmosphere breathable. Holding on to the exposed joist with one hand, he leaned down.

'Feel for me.'

An interval: then her hand brushed his arm. Obtaining a wrist grip, he held her firm, steered her hand to the joist. 'Grab hold of that. Got it? Anchor yourself. I'm leaving go.'

She started coughing, but he could sense that she was secure. He let go. Biffing with his palm, he reached the limit of the boarding that had been ravaged by woodworm; switching to the other side, he opened up a few more inches. Thrusting farther, his fingers met a spongy resistance.

In revulsion he recoiled: then he argued it out. Sponge. Foam rubber. Carpet underlay. He called down: 'I'm going to try pulling myself through. Stay still—keep holding on.'

Coughing, he moved his head about until he found smoke-free air. With lungs replenished, he curled the fingers of both hands about the joist and raised himself.

The soft barrier pressed on his head. As he strained, it lifted; a chink of light appeared.

Both his feet were clear of the topmost crate. All the pressure was on his arms and shoulders. He swung his legs in a vain search for purchase. The carpet sank, forcing him downwards.

An arm went around his thighs. Irene had perceived the problem and was doing what she could. It was sufficient to provide equipoise, gave him the lift he sought to return to the assault, to elevate the carpet until the chink of radiance became a shaft and he could work both shoulders through the hole to support himself by his elbows on top of the boards. He paused a moment.

The crushing burden of the tautened carpet seemed to be driving his neck into his shoulders. Again he lifted: the load defied him stubbornly. The thought came to him that the carpet-edges must be tacked.

For a second he felt his muscles sag.

The light stealing beneath, so near to his face, provided the vital spur. Too close to give up now. Taking a long-drawn breath, harnessing all the strength of his sinew, he heaved fiercely.

With a tearing sound the edge of the carpet left the floor. Relieved of pressure, he hauled up his body and legs, spreadeagled himself across the boards with the carpet sinking back on top of him. He lay gasping for breath.

Below, Irene was coughing. He extended both arms into the hole.

'Hands,' he commanded.

Slender fingers slipped into his. He found her left wrist, and then her right: but under the carpet his movements were cramped. A steady upwards pull was out of the question.

'I'll have to leave go. Shift the carpet. Can you hold on?'

He released one wrist, felt it touch his arm as she searched for a new grip on the boarding. She tugged away her other hand. 'Okay,' she said chokingly.

Straightening his body, he rolled.

The space widened between carpet and wall. Light flooded in. Flickering light, the colour of a blood-orange. He fought his way through the gap. He was clear. Staggering to his feet, he heard the roaring in his ears.

He turned. Smoke was billowing up the staircase, uncoiling towards him: no flame as yet. Stumbling away from it to the window at the end of the corridor, he knelt and tore at the carpet-edge.

It was wall-to-wall. No tacks; but the sponge under-lay had adhered to the floorboards, fusing into a mass. He tried from the other corner. Part of it rolled back, then snagged: he kicked it free. Suddenly the carpet lifted easily: more woodworm, more dust, less adhesion. Getting behind it, he heaved frantically.

The smoke was building up, eddying towards the window. The bulk he was pushing became unwieldy, hampered by contact with the walls, veering off course as it accumulated unevenly. Here and there the under-lay was stuck: he ripped the pile away.

Half the distance covered. Smoke around him: he tried holding his breath. Exertion defeated him; he had to pant, to choke away the fumes. He stayed low. A final heave. The ragged hole lay exposed.

Irene's hand came through. Seizing it, he knelt, caught her by an armpit, hauled her up and out. She was coughing uncontrollably.

An air-pocket beneath the smoke came to his aid. Snatching a gulp, he began pulling her towards the window.

Above the roaring came a sharper noise, a shattering of glass and woodwork. He turned to peer. Smoke enveloped them, blotting out all vision.

'Shove up the nozzle then, Graham.'

With the last of his wind, Larkin called feebly.

'Hold it, Graham! There's someone inside. Tell 'em not yet. We'll have to—'

CHAPTER XXI

SMUT ENTERED the room with Caroline and two copies of the *Miltham Mail*.

'Thought you might like to see,' he said diffidently, 'how we handled it.'

Larkin examined the layout with a critical eye. 'Better than the nationals.'

'See, love? Expert appreciation. Didn't I say there was still a place for the one-man show?'

'No,' she retorted, 'that wasn't what you said. You said, I'll let old Jim see he should never have quit the local patch where the real journalism is. Get your facts right.' She sat on the bed. 'How are you, Jim?'

'Now that I've stopped coughing,' he explained, 'there's just a few nightmares and the odd fit of delirium to contend with. What about Irene?'

'She's grand. You'll see her tonight when you come to dinner. Off home tomorrow, aren't you?'

'That's the plan.' Larkin nodded towards the trolley at his bedside. 'I've decided it'll be cheaper than the hourly phone conversations, of a peculiar incoherence, that I'm having at present with my wife. Less strenuous too. Each time she calls, I feel I have to sound larger than life, better than well, in case she starts packing.'

'I know *exactly* how she feels,' asserted Caroline. 'The things she must have read in the papers . . . I do hope she'll be all right.'

'Luckily,' said Larkin, 'she's too furious to be anything else.'

'Don't you believe it. That's just to cover up.'

'Yes,' he said penitently, 'I believe you're right.'

'You get home, Jim, and show her you're still in one piece.'

'What a bloody story,' said Smut, staring at his own front page. 'Poor old Hilda, silly old cow.'

'She wasn't old,' said Caroline. 'Just potty. I can't help feeling glad . . .' She stopped.

'That she didn't get out of the Stag?' said Larkin gently.

'Well—it's sort of appropriate, isn't it?'

'If you care for that sort of suitability,' remarked Smut.

'It was her life, after all.'

'To say nothing of her death.' Smut handed Larkin a half-bottle of brandy with a wink. 'You've heard all the gory details, Jim, I take it?'

'Some I've heard, a lot I've read, a few I've made up. I'll fill in from the *Mail*.'

'All you'll find in there, old sport, is what you've recently experienced at uncomfortably first hand. I am now in a position—' Smut assumed a lordly air —'to cover the blanks. What do you want to know?'

'Er . . . well. How much did Mrs Thorpe suspect?'

'The worst. She'd guessed what her sister had done. Wanted to protect her but didn't know how. She—'

'How could she have guessed?' demanded Caroline.

'I'm not saying she knew just what had occurred. She didn't, obviously. But when Maisie and the Sandersons went missing and Hilda jumped in the stream—'

'She really was suicidal?'

'Sure. No fake about that. Thanks to his hiking activities, Jim was on hand to pull her out, but they reckon the shock of the plunge brought on Hilda's amnesia—likewise genuine. So her sister couldn't get out of her what had happened. Nobody could. All she knew was, it was something bad. Then the night before last—'

'Mossop had another go at her,' said Larkin.

'Went bald-headed for Hilda. He was convinced you and she were in cahoots. Something that was said must have clicked in Hilda's brain—or maybe her memory was coming back anyhow. Or it could even have been the sight of you, Jim. In any event, after you'd all left she must have decided she badly wanted to get back to the Stag to see that things were under control.'

Caroline frowned.

'You mean she'd remembered by then that she'd poisoned three people a few days before, and she wanted to check on the arrangements?'

'It's a way of putting it, love.'

'How,' asked Larkin, 'did she get out of the cottage?'

'First she locked her sister in the larder. When Sergeant Willis came running to see what the row was about, she sloshed him from behind with—you'll never guess—the rolling pin. He's still off duty.'

'You surprise me.' Larkin put a hand tenderly to his own neck.

'After that she simply filched the car keys from her sister's bag and drove into town. She brought her own set of Stag keys which her sister had shoved in a drawer.'

Caroline said with rounded eyes, 'Was Mrs Thorpe in the larder all night?'

'Right up to Breakfast Special. It's a bit isolated, that cottage. No one heard her shrieking: not till the milkman arrived.'

'The milkman,' Larkin said significantly.

'Yeah, Jim, I hadn't forgotten.' Unstopping the

brandy, Smut splashed some into three cups. He distributed them. Planking himself down at the foot of the bed, he nursed his drink with affection. 'Yesterday afternoon, as you suggested, I drove round to the depot and, weary as I was—'

'It's a hard life,' quavered Caroline, deadpan.

'Well, granted I hadn't been clamped in a kiln all night, but it *was* press day. Anyway I nailed Ron Appleby in a quiet corner and showed him the bit of paper. At first he was Vehement in his Denials. When I said you'd seen him drop it, he started to crack in places: when I'd said a few other things about showing it to his wife, he fell apart. You were right, Jim. He and Maisie had been Seeing One Another. Apparently they had this system—'

'My husband,' announced Caroline, 'has taken careful notes.'

'You bet. The system was, on prearranged days he'd take his round at a gallop and on his way back he'd drive his van into the Stag courtyard, where Maisie would be waiting near the kitchen door. This was generally about four, when things were slack and the Sandersons were resting. Into the van she'd dart, off to a quiet spot he'd motor and—' Smut raised both hands. 'Then back he'd run her to somewhere quiet on the town fringe, and Stagwards she'd stroll while he showed up at the depot. This happened about once a week.'

'And he used to hide notes in a wall crevice near the kitchen door, to let her know it was on?'

'The previous day,' Smut confirmed. 'And as ill-luck would have it, on the very morning of your arrival—'

'He'd stuffed a note in the usual place.'

'Then later he heard they'd all gone missing. That shook him. More so when he kept getting quizzed by narks and newsmen. Unnerved, he was. Didn't even think of the note till days later. Then it hit him. If Maisie hadn't collected, there it was, stuck in the wall, in his handwriting: *Pick you up tomorrow, Ron.* What if it was found?'

'Retribution,' breathed Caroline. 'That's what.'

'We're not here to make moral judgments, love, as the magistrate said to the probation officer. Point is, this is what Jim spotted him doing that evening—getting it back.'

'Then he goes and drops it,' said Caroline with contempt. 'He's not even a clever bastard.'

'He sees that now. Mrs Ron Appleby, I feel, will have an impeccably-behaved husband on her hands for a year or two.'

'Doesn't he even feel a bit sorry about Maisie?' she demanded.

'Oh sure. We all do, don't we?' Smut quirked a rueful mouth at Larkin. 'Feeling fit, Jim? I said I'd run you to headquarters.'

As Larkin was signing his written statement, Chief Inspector Mossop made an impassive appearance.

'Owe you an apology.'

Larkin shook his head.

'Commiseration, then. Plus congratulations on a lucky escape. When they finally got to that brick tomb—'

'Not now,' said Larkin hastily.

'No. We—er—did manage to get them identified.'

Mossop's fingers drummed the counter. Larkin pushed the signed sheets across to the waiting sergeant.

'Come in a moment,' said the chief inspector.

The room was as warm as ever. Stationing himself at

the window, Mossop gazed out at the gaunt-foliaged patch that it overlooked; then turned away as though tired of the sight.

He said abruptly, 'I'm under fire.'

'I know the feeling.'

'The Press boys ... you've probably read. Why wasn't the storeroom found earlier? This kind of thing.'

'Easy to talk.'

'I don't know.' Mossop looked tired. 'A closer search of the building ... Maybe I didn't treat the entire thing seriously enough.'

'Perhaps nobody did.' Larkin eyed him thoughtfully. 'I seem to remember much Press comment to the effect that it had all the makings of a gimmick.'

'That's *right*.' Mossop cheered up. Grew pensive again. 'Planning to write anything yourself?'

'It's my trade.'

The chief inspector estimated the remark. Looking at his desk, he said, 'The full unvarnished story, I suppose.'

'Oh, I shall mention my own near-implication, for what it's worth.' Larkin paused. 'But I don't propose to be too solemn about it.'

Their eyes met. Reluctantly Mossop permitted himself a half-smile.

'I doubt if one can ask for more than that.'

'As a matter of interest,' Larkin said with a new briskness, 'how is it that no one came forward to tell you of the storeroom? Wasn't it known about?'

Becoming a policeman again, Mossop returned to his desk.

'Charles Barrett contacted us this morning. Ex-owner of the Stag, now runs a hotel in Norfolk. He and his wife have been cruising on the Broads—first heard about this affair on today's early radio bulletin. He told me about the store.'

'When was it built?'

'Been there donkey's years. That is, the space has. Originally it was one huge inglenook, but when he took over the inn, twenty-odd years ago, Barrett had this idea of dividing part of it off and using it as a wine-cellar—'

'Next to a chimney?'

'They were going to install a big electric fire. Nuts on electricity, he was. Everything push-button, easy to run. They closed the Stag for a fortnight, called in a Plymouth firm and had the work done. Skilfully done, too. It was—'

'How did they make the door?'

'They hung the brickwork on a pivoting steel frame that swung open or shut when you threw the kitchen switch. The edges were made irregular. What with that and the roughness of the brickwork generally, when it was flush you couldn't see the joins unless you knew where to look. Also it was solid to the touch. The Press,' said Mossop defensively, 'can say what they like, but personally I don't condemn my chaps for missing it.'

'If it comes to that,' said Larkin, 'I was chatting to a colleague before the Press conference and he was resting his great meaty hand right on it.'

'Proves my point. A lovely piece of work. There was just one small deficiency . . .'

'No interior switch.'

'And of course, the day after it was installed the obvious happened: Mrs Barrett got herself entombed. As a joke he shut the door on her while she was inside. That wouldn't have mattered terribly, but would you believe, before he could open it again the power failed. Fault in a local substation. Took half an hour to rectify; by the time it came on again—'

'Mrs B. was in hysterics?'

'After she'd recovered, she vetoed any further use of it. Made him disconnect the switch, told Hilda to say nothing about it to anyone. They wrote it off. Kept to log fires instead, all very traditional, and stored the wine in the basement.'

'And when the Sandersons took over?'

'Barrett never mentioned it to them. His wife told him not to: she had a horror of it.'

'So how did the switch become reconnected?'

'Hilda,' said Mossop simply. 'Faced with three dead people over the wineglasses, she must have turned off the power and joined up the wires. She'd have known what to do. According to Barrett, she watched him sever them at the time.'

Larkin digested the information.

'What was it,' he murmured, 'that brought on this sudden compulsion to kill the three of them?'

Mossop looked serious. 'From what you've told us, and from what her sister has managed to say, it rather appears that Hilda had some form of hang-up over young Maisie.'

'But—'

'Nothing lesbian, I don't mean that. But it seems she'd got increasingly worked up over the last few weeks about the relationship between Maisie and the Sandersons. Here again, Mrs Thorpe's not apparently suggesting anything improper—but I shall be talking again to Mrs Charles, Maisie's aunt, in the hope that she's more forthcoming now that the worst is known. It may be that Hilda had grown very fond of the girl, as a middle-aged spinster might, and became jealous of the Sandersons.'

'Who were treating Maisie like a daughter,' said Larkin meditatively.

'Yes—and that's an interesting point,' said Mossop abruptly.

'What is?'

'Just a remark that Mrs Thorpe let slip. Something about a fixation on Hilda's part that Maisie was her own grandchild.' Mossop pondered. 'Further inquiries,' he said at last, 'are definitely indicated. You can quote me on that.'

CHAPTER XXII

CLOSING THE LOUNGE DOOR with a firm hand, Philip Potter stifled the lively hubbub from the bar. Pouring two glassfuls of Drambuie from the bottle on the tray, he handed one to Larkin and took the other to an adjoining chintz-covered chair into which he sank.

'No one ever comes in here. Least of all after lunch. Too shut off.' He looked round vaguely. 'We were thinking of knocking the wall down, adding it to the bar. May get around to it some time. Meanwhile,' he said, arranging one leg across the other, 'it's a good place for a quiet chat.'

'You're certain you don't mind?'

Potter lifted a hand, drank and shook his head. 'I believe you've earned the right—'

'I'm entitled to no more than the next man.'

'That's a matter of opinion.' Potter brooded over his glass. 'It's a long time ago now.'

Larkin produced pipe and tobacco tin. With a sense of luxury despite the frigidity of the room, he commenced to pack the bowl.

Potter spoke as though starting a lecture to a student assembly. 'Forty years or so ago,' he told the ceiling, 'these two young people had an affair lasting a few weeks. He was twenty, she was sixteen. It was violent while it lasted.'

He was silent for a space.

Larkin struck a match. 'But it soon ended?'

The older man started. 'The family pressure on his side was very great. She wasn't considered—' He paused '—his type. In those days that was still important. Is now, of course; only people proclaim otherwise until it's too late. They can afford to. Breakups don't matter any more. At that time the situation was regarded as very fraught, and the pair were duly separated. The young woman went away to relatives and later had a child.'

Larkin ignited the tobacco. 'Girl or boy?'

'A girl. Meanwhile the young man remained here and married—someone of his own station in life. They had a son. Several years went by, and then the young unmarried mother came back to the town to live with her parents. In point of fact—' Potter waved an arm— 'they had a small house just at the back of here. It's Hilda I'm speaking of, as you'll have gathered.'

'Yes. Did she bring her daughter?'

'She was left, it seems, to be brought up by the relatives. Hilda went to work at the Stag.'

'With the Barretts?'

'Their predecessors. Mathers, I think was the name.'

'Hazarding a guess,' said Larkin, puffing busily, 'do I take it that before long she was causing embarrassment to the young man and his family?'

'You do, and she was. To him, anyway. He paid her regular amounts towards her child's expenses, but what she seemed set upon was getting her own back. She'd find excuses to accost them, pester the man, drop veiled hints to his wife. Just as it was becoming intolerable her father died, and shortly afterwards her mother. This knocked her out for a while.'

'And after that she sold the house?'

'Her sister, Mrs Thorpe, who'd been widowed by then, helped her dispose of it. Hilda went to live with her, and gradually she seemed to put the past behind.

She evidently became resigned to spinsterhood. Her work at the Stag was her life.'

Potter glanced at Larkin's glass, saw that it was full and gave him a searching look. 'Clear so far?'

'Very.' Larkin applied a second match to the supine mass in his pipe-bowl. 'What became of her daughter.'

'Left school, worked as a solicitor's typist, got fed up, married at twenty-three, had a baby girl. Two years later, ran off with the insurance man. Husband walked out, never came back. Two-year-old daughter went to his sister.'

'So Hilda did have a grandchild. Her name wasn't Sarah, by any chance?'

'That was her daughter's name.' Potter hesitated. 'The grand-daughter was called Maisie.'

Blowing smoke aside, Larkin looked at him.

'And the aunt is Mrs Charles?'

Potter nodded.

'Being a widow herself, she had a struggle to bring Maisie up. She got some financial help—all he could afford—from the girl's grandfather, who'd managed to keep track of events. And seven years ago, when that cottage of mine in Main Street became vacant, it was offered to her at a nominal rent. She was glad to take it.'

'With the grandfather making up the deficit?'

Potter inclined his head.

Larkin smoked thoughtfully. 'Did Hilda know who they were?'

'Yes. The grandfather told her. He thought it would be a consolation to her to know that her grandchild was being looked after—but it proved a disastrous mistake.'

'In what way?'

The lounge door opened with a rattle. Gavin Foster

peered in, said 'Sorry, Jim,' and withdrew, elaborately discreet.

Potter gazed for some moments at the door before resuming. 'Hilda became possessive. In a muddled sort of way, I think, she saw Maisie as Sarah . . . more as her lost daughter than as the grandchild. She was in her fifties now, Hilda, and you must remember she'd lived a rather—frustrated life. And mentally she was never strong. In retrospect, I suppose that having Maisie around, knowing who she was but having no real claim to her apart from blood, was the worst thing that could have happened to her.'

Larkin sipped his Drambuie. 'Was it she who engineered Maisie's job at the Stag?'

'Well, the Sandersons were looking for someone— this was just before the fishing slump—and Maisie had just left school and was keen on domestic science, so I guess it seemed tailor-made. I certainly wouldn't think Hilda was averse to the idea: at least not at first.'

'But later?'

'Then complications set in. To start with, Hilda tried to smother Maisie with affection and expected the girl to return it. Maisie for her part, not unnaturally, wanted very little to do with her. She was quite unaware of their relationship. To her she was just old Hilda, the drudge of the inn, who'd been there close on forty years and seemed set for another forty. And what was worse—'

'The Sandersons?' prompted Larkin.

'Yes indeed, the Sandersons. Being childless themselves, they very soon developed a great fondness for Maisie. They told me this, not realizing—'

'Did Maisie return their affection?' Larkin inquired as the older man stopped again.

'To a great extent, I believe. No doubt to her they were the parents she'd never had. They were an exceedingly nice couple, you know.' Once more Potter's voice trailed off. Staring at his glass, he put it mechanically to his lips and lowered it again.

'The fishing slump . . . ?' Larkin ventured.

'What? Ah yes. When that came along, we both had to reduce staff. In the case of the Stag—'

'It was Maisie who was kept on, and Hilda who went over to half-days.'

'Precisely. And this amounted to a double slap in the face for poor Hilda. Here was Maisie being wrested from her, quite unwittingly, by her employers—and on top of that, here was her beloved Stag being partly closed to her in favour of the newcomer. Can you wonder if her mind was buffeted? I believe there came an explosion.'

'Caused by something in particular?'

'We can only guess. But I can't help recalling something Sanderson said to me a week or two previously. We're thinking of adopting Maisie, he said. Legally, he meant. I said to him, You'd give her your name, make her your heiress? And he laughed and said, Yes, all our princely fortune—but all we're really after is to feel that we're a family. So I asked him, what about Mrs Charles? To which he said that technically Maisie was of age, but of course they'd ask Mrs Charles for permission and her blessing. Now I don't know,' said Potter, shifting in his chair, 'whether what they had in mind was a practical proposition: but somehow I picture them, on the morning of the day you arrived, Mr Larkin, having a little celebration.'

'A celebration?'

'Perhaps they'd put it to Maisie and she'd agreed,

and to Mrs Charles and she'd approved. I'm still guessing. But I picture them in the lounge of the inn that morning, discussing the plan, deciding to drink to it. I imagine the conversation. Fetch in the sherry, Hilda—Maisie's going to become a Sanderson. Pour out four glasses, there's a dear. I see Hilda getting a bottle from the basement. Pouring it in the kitchen. There's rat poison to hand in a cupboard. Cyanide pellets: the ones we gave the Sandersons to help them out . . .'

Larkin observed the other man's face. It was turned towards the carpeted floor; his eyes were half-closed. His voice had dipped to a murmur.

Very gently Larkin said, 'The man you've been talking about, the grandfather of Maisie . . . he's a great friend of yours?'

For some moments Potter sat motionless. Slowly his head began to shake.

'No, he's not a friend,' he said to the floor, 'but I've known him all my life.'

Presently Larkin knocked out and stowed his pipe. Rising, he looked down at the huddled figure in the chintz armchair. It remained still. He walked to the door and opened it. The bar noise leapt in. He looked round.

'I hope the fish come back,' he said.

Smut brought in the coffee tray. He served Irene first, with anxious deference to her bandaged right arm.

'Manage, chicken? Like a smaller cup?'

'Smut, don't be a goof. I've just dealt with a three-course meal, haven't I?'

'It's his rug he's bothered about,' Caroline said realistically. 'Cost him two quid eighty in a sale.'

'Shan't spill any, Smut, I promise.'

'I don't mind,' he said with dignity, 'if you chuck it all over the wallpaper. Keep it away from Jim, though. He's Satanic when roused. Sprain anyone's wrist at the drop of a hat.'

Irene sent Larkin a small smile. 'He meant well.'

'Did well, too,' said Caroline. 'Now can we drop the whole beastly subject. Leaving early tomorrow, Jim?'

'The moment I'm alive.'

'We'll be sorry to see you go.'

'Well, I'll be back, of course, for the inquest.'

'Oh God.'

'See, love,' said Smut, patting her arm. 'Try to bend it away, it whangs back at you. Hey Jim, tell you what. How much for the serial rights?'

'In the *Miltham Mail*?' Larkin considered. 'We can arrange terms on that. In the meantime, what about *My Ordeal By Brick And Fire, by Hotel Heroine*?'

'Already set up,' scoffed Smut. 'Next week's issue. Usual rates, chicken, okay?'

'She doesn't want to talk about it.'

'Yes, I do, Carrie. I'm not to bottle it up.' She consulted Larkin, who nodded. 'Usual rates? I don't know about that.'

'Here it comes,' groaned her brother-in-law. 'For first-hand stories the price goes up, huh? You've been reading—'

'I wasn't talking about that. I meant you may be losing your contact at the Royal.'

She looked challengingly at her sister, who rose to nibble.

'You're not leaving?'

'I've decided,' said Irene, 'that hotel work can be dicey at times. So I'm going to try my hand as a social

187

worker. Plymouth or somewhere. It's what I've always wanted to do, after all.'

'How about Mum and Dad?'

'We've talked it over. They say they can get along.'

'Of course they can,' said Caroline forcefully. 'I've always thought so. Smut and I can keep an eye on them. You make off, dear: get socializing. It'll suit you.'

'Thanks, Carrie.' Setting down her cup, Irene leaned across to give Larkin a swift kiss. 'And thanks, Jim.'

'Hey, hey,' said Smut suspiciously. 'What's all this?'

'Just a spot of innocent collusion,' Larkin told him.

'There's no such thing. Try telling that to Bunty. Ho hum. More coffee, Jim? Free from toxic additives, I guarantee.'

'If it'll help to keep me conscious.' Larkin yawned, and yawned again. 'All I seem to want to do at the moment is lie around, and rest, and sleep . . .'

Smut eyed him sardonically. 'What you need,' he said, 'is a holiday.'

RECENT CRIME CLUB TITLES

July - November 1974

JULY

How to Live Dangerously
JOAN FLEMING
'After sixty-five years of age, live dangerously,' the Oxford Regius Professor of Medicine had publicly advised. Pendle Hill, ex-Naval Intelligence and an Oxford resident, decided to do just that. Unfortunately his landlady had other ideas.

A Question of Degree ROY LEWIS
The woman whose body was found down a South Wales coal mine had been in search of a missing husband, whom she had found. But Inspector Crow did not believe the husband's story. Strange events were to prove him strangely right.

Holiday with a Vengeance
RITCHIE PERRY
Pawson's offer of a free holiday in the Bahamas sounded to Philis just too good to be true. And it was. Philis soon found himself at the head of a guerrilla force intent on overthrowing a dictator – which was not Pawson's idea at all.

AUGUST

Death by Hoax LIONEL BLACK
The hoaxes in a small seaside town seemed just hoaxes – until one of them proved for real. Only it was no hoax but the cover for a carefully planned murder. And there was more violence to come.

Mistakenly in Mallorca
RODERIC JEFFRIES
Elvina Woods's death in Mallorca was sudden and accidental. When her great-nephew decided, for reasons of his own, to conceal it, he let himself in for more than he bargained for.

Phantom Holiday MARTIN RUSSELL
The Devonshire inn where reporter Jim Larkin arrived to spend his holiday was quiet – too quiet. In perfect order but empty of staff and guests. Soon the nationals were calling it 'the *Mary Celeste* on dry land' and Larkin was in it up to the neck.

SEPTEMBER

Poirot's Early Cases AGATHA CHRISTIE

Eighteen stories, many never previously published in book form, of the early cases of Hercule Poirot, one of the world's most celebrated detectives. A treasure trove of vintage Christie.

The Man in the Sopwith Camel
MICHAEL BUTTERWORTH

Ernest Kitteridge worked in a bank and banked in a Sopwith Camel. In fancy an air ace of World War I, he dreamed of life on a Pacific isle. Bizarre circumstances suddenly put his dreams within his grasp, and the result is the delightful, dotty story of how he took to crime.

The Motive HARRY CARMICHAEL

All the indications were that Robert Heseltine, consultant surgeon, had drowned when he jumped off a Dorset cliff. But when Quinn of the *Morning Post* and Piper, insurance assessor, delve into his background, his disappearance takes on a terrible significance.

You Can Help Me MAISIE BIRMINGHAM

A residential social settlement in London's East End, in the immediate hinterland of Petticoat Lane, is the setting for this classic whodunit featuring crime among do-gooders, written by the wife of an ex-Warden of Toynbee Hall.

OCTOBER

Alive and Dead ELIZABETH FERRARS

Of all the cases Martha Crayle had dealt with in her work for unmarried mothers, none was more puzzling than that of Amanda Hassall. For Amanda wasn't unmarried – and thereby hung a crime.

Unfair Exchange MARIAN BABSON

Fanny was not an endearing child and Zita hadn't wanted to be lumbered with her. All the same, when Fanny was kidnapped Zita could hardly help becoming embroiled on her behalf, and soon she was in peril of her life.

NOVEMBER

Slyboots PAT FLOWER

The alliance of youthful Rick Coleman and middle-aged Emily Sutton was based on mutual self-interest. It took them across Europe in pursuit of a fortune and had an altogether unexpected ending in the Australian bush.

Death of an Old Goat
ROBERT BARNARD

The murder of an aged English professor on a visit to an Australian university in the outback involves the unscrupulous local inspector with both the academic and the grazing communities in this splendid send-up of the academic world down under.